The Hollow

Agatha Christie

A SAMUEL FRENCH ACTING EDITION

SAMUEL
FRENCH

FOUNDED 1830

SAMUELFRENCH.COM
SAMUELFRENCH-LONDON.CO.UK

ISBN 978-0-573-70239-6

www.SamuelFrench.com
www.SamuelFrench-London.co.uk

MUSIC USE NOTE

Licensees are solely responsible for obtaining formal written permission from copyright owners to use copyrighted music in the performance of this play and are strongly cautioned to do so. If no such permission is obtained by the licensee, then the licensee must use only original music that the licensee owns and controls. Licensees are solely responsible and liable for all music clearances and shall indemnify the copyright owners of the play(s) and their licensing agent, Samuel French, against any costs, expenses, losses and liabilities arising from the use of music by licensees. Please contact the appropriate music licensing authority in your territory for the rights to any incidental music.

IMPORTANT BILLING AND CREDIT REQUIREMENTS

If you have obtained performance rights to this title, please refer to your licensing agreement for important billing and credit requirements.

THE HOLLOW was first presented by Peter Saunders at the Fortune Theatre, London on 7 June 1951. The performance was directed by Hubert Gregg. The cast was as follows:

HENRIETTA ANGKATELL . . . . Beryl Baxter

SIR HENRY ANGKATELL, K.C.B. . . . . George Thorpe

LADY ANGKATELL . . . . Jeanne de Casalis

MIDGE HARVEY . . . . Jessica Spencer

GUDGEON . . . . A. J. Brown

EDWARD ANGKATELL . . . . Colin Douglas

DORIS . . . . Patricia Jones

GERDA CRISTOW . . . . Joan Newell

JOHN CRISTOW, M.D., F.R.C.P. . . . . Ernest Clark

VERONICA CRAYE . . . . Dianne Foster

INSPECTOR COLQUHOUN, C.I.D. . . . . Martin Wyldech

DETECTIVE SERGEANT PENNY . . . . Shaw Taylor

The play was subsequently transferred to the Ambassador's Theatre.

CHARACTERS

HENRIETTA ANGKATELL
SIR HENRY ANGKATELL, K.C.B.
LADY ANGKATELL
MIDGE HARVEY
GUDGEON
EDWARD ANGKATELL
DORIS
GERDA CRISTOW
JOHN CRISTOW, M.D., F.R.C.P.
VERONICA CRAYE
INSPECTOR COLQUHOUN, C.I.D.
DETECTIVE SERGEANT PENNY

SETTING

The action of the play passes in the garden room of Sir Henry Angkatell's house, The Hollow, about eighteen miles from London

ACT ONE

A Friday afternoon in early September

ACT TWO

Scene I: Saturday morning
Scene II: Later the same day

ACT THREE

The following Monday morning. The lights are lowered during Act Three to denote the passing of one hour.

ACT ONE

(Scene – The garden room of **SIR HENRY ANGKATELL***'s house, The Hollow, about eighteen miles from London. A Friday afternoon in early September.)*

(It is an informal room, but furnished with taste. Back centre, up three steps, there are French windows opening on to a terrace with a low wall at the far side. Beyond the wall there is a view of the wooded hillside on which the house is built. There are smaller French windows, up one step, centre of the wall right, leading to the garden and giving a view of dense shrubbery. A door down left leads to the other parts of the house. There is a large alcove in the back wall left of the French windows. The entrance to this is arched and a heavy curtain in the archway closes it off from the rest of the room. The back wall of the alcove is fitted with well filled, built-in bookshelves and furnished with a small table on which stands a silver bowl of roses. A piece of statuary can be supposed to stand in the alcove though not visible to the audience. The fireplace is centre of the wall left and there are well-filled, built-in bookshelves in the walls right of the French windows up centre and below the French windows right. There is a small writing table down right, on which stands a small table-lamp and a telephone. A small chair is set at the table and a waste-paper basket stands below it. Above the writing table there is a pedestal on which stands a piece of abstract statuary. There is a table with a table-lamp on it below the bookshelves up right. A small table with a radio receiver stands above the fireplace. There is an armchair up left centre, and a comfortable sofa right centre. Below the sofa stands a small, circular coffee table. A pouffe near the hearth completes the

furniture. The room is carpeted and gay curtains hang at the windows. In addition to the table-lamps, the room is lit at night by an electric candle-lamp wall-bracket left of the French windows up centre, and small electric candle-lamps on the mantelpiece. One or two miniatures decorate the walls, and over the mantelpiece there is a fine picture depicting the idyllic scene of a Georgian house with columns, set in woodlands. The light switch and bell-push are in the wall below the fireplace. There is also a switch controlling the light in the alcove, right of the arch. Two wall vases, filled with flowers, decorate the side walls of the french windows up centre.)

(See the Ground Plan)

(When the curtain rises, it is a fine afternoon and all the French windows stand open. **SIR HENRY ANGKATELL**, *K.C.B., a distinguished-looking, elderly man, is seated at the right end of the sofa, reading "The Times."* **HENRIETTA ANGKATELL** *is on the terrace outside the French windows up centre, standing at a tall sculptor's stand, modelling in clay. She is a handsome young woman of about thirty-three, dressed in good country tweeds and over them a painter's overall. She advances and retreats towards her creation once or twice then enters up centre and moves to the coffee table below the sofa. There is a smear of clay on her nose and she is frowning.)*

HENRIETTA. *(as she enters)* Damn and damn and damn!

SIR HENRY. *(looking up)* Not going well?

HENRIETTA. *(taking a cigarette from the box on the coffee table)* What misery it is to be a sculptor.

SIR HENRY. It must be. I always thought you had to have models for this sort of thing.

HENRIETTA. It's an abstract piece I'm modelling, darling.

SIR HENRY. What – *(he points with distaste to the piece of modern sculpture on the pedestal right)* – like that?

HENRIETTA. *(crossing to the mantelpiece)* Anything interesting in *The Times*? *(She lights her cigarette with the table lighter on the mantelpiece.)*

SIR HENRY. Lots of people dead. *(He looks at* **HENRIETTA**.*)* You've got clay on your nose.

HENRIETTA. What?

SIR HENRY. *Clay* – on your *nose*.

HENRIETTA. *(looking in the mirror on the mantelpiece; vaguely)* Oh, so I have. *(She rubs her nose, then her forehead, turns and moves left centre)*

SIR HENRY. Now it's all over your face.

HENRIETTA. *(moving up centre; exasperated)* Does it matter, darling?

SIR HENRY. Evidently not.

*(***HENRIETTA*** goes on to the terrace up centre and resumes work.* **LADY ANGKATELL** *enters right. She is a very charming and aristocratic looking woman aged about sixty, completely vague, but with a lot of personality. She is apparently in the middle of a conversation.)*

LADY ANGKATELL. *(crossing above the sofa to the fireplace)* Oh dear, oh dear! If it isn't one thing it's another. Did I leave a mole-trap in here? *(She picks up the mole-trap from the mantelpiece and eases centre)* Ah yes – there it is. The worst of moles is – you never know where they are going to pop up next. People are quite right when they say that nature in the mild is seldom raw. *(She crosses below the sofa to right.)* Don't you think I'm right, Henry?

SIR HENRY. I couldn't say, my dear, unless I know what you're talking about.

LADY ANGKATELL. I'm going to pursue them quite ruthlessly – I really am.

(Her voice dies away as she exits right.)

HENRIETTA. *(looking in through the French window up centre)* What did Lucy say?

SIR HENRY. Nothing much. Just being Lucyish. I say, it's half past six.

HENRIETTA. I'll have to stop and clean myself up. They're all coming by car, I suppose? *(She drapes a damp cloth over her work.)*

SIR HENRY. All except Midge. She's coming by Green Line bus. Ought to be here by now.

HENRIETTA. Darling Midge. She is nice. Heaps nicer than any of us, don't you think? *(She pushes the stand out of sight right of the terrace.)*

SIR HENRY. I must have notice of that question.

HENRIETTA. *(moving centre; laughing)* Well, less eccentric, anyway. There's something very sane about Midge. *(She rubs her hands on her overall.)*

SIR HENRY. *(indignantly)* I'm perfectly sane, thank you.

HENRIETTA. *(removing her overall and looking at **SIR HENRY**)* Ye-es – perhaps *you* are. *(She puts her overall over the back of the armchair left centre.)*

SIR HENRY. *(smiling)* As sane as anyone can be that has to live with Lucy, bless her heart. *(He laughs.)*

*(**HENRIETTA** laughs, crosses to the mantelpiece and puts her cigarette ash in the ashtray.)*

(He puts his newspaper on the coffee table. Worried.) You know, Henrietta, I'm getting worried about Lucy.

HENRIETTA. Worried? Why?

SIR HENRY. Lucy doesn't realize there are certain things she can't do.

HENRIETTA. *(looking in the mirror)* I don't think I quite know what you mean. *(She pats her hair.)*

SIR HENRY. She's always got away with things. I don't suppose any other woman in the world could have flouted the traditions of Government House as she did. *(He takes his pipe from his pocket.)* Most governors' wives have to toe the line of convention. But not Lucy! Oh dear me, no! She played merry hell with precedence at dinner parties – and that, my dear Henrietta, is the blackest of crimes.

(HENRIETTA turns.)

(He pats his pockets, feeling for his tobacco pouch.) She put deadly enemies next to each other. She ran riot over the colour question. And instead of setting everyone at loggerheads, I'm damned if she didn't get away with it.

(HENRIETTA picks up the tobacco jar from the mantelpiece, crosses and hands it to SIR HENRY.)

Oh, thank you. It's that trick of hers – always smiling at people and looking so sweet and helpless. Servants are the same – she gives them any amount of trouble and they simply adore her.

HENRIETTA. I know what you mean. *(She sits on the sofa at the left end.)* Things you wouldn't stand from anyone else, you feel they are quite all right if Lucy does them. What is it? Charm? Hypnotism?

SIR HENRY. *(filling his pipe)* I don't know. She's always been the same from a girl. But you know, Henrietta, it's growing on her. She doesn't seem to realize there *are* limits. I really believe Lucy would feel she could get away with *murder.*

HENRIETTA. *(rising and picking up the piece of clay from the carpet)* Darling Henry, you and Lucy are angels letting me make my messes here – treading clay into your carpet. *(She crosses and puts the piece of clay in the waste-paper basket down right.)* When I had that fire at my studio, I thought it was the end of everything – it was sweet of you to let me move in on you.

SIR HENRY. My dear, we're proud of you. Why, I've just been reading a whole article about you and your show in *The Times.*

HENRIETTA. *(crossing to the coffee table and picking up "The Times")* Where?

SIR HENRY. Top of the page. There, I believe. Of course, I don't profess to know much about it myself.

HENRIETTA. *(reading)* "The most significant piece of the year." Oh, what gup! I must go and wash.

(She drops the paper on the sofa, crosses, picks up her overall and exits hurriedly left. SIR HENRY *rises, puts the papers and tobacco on the coffee table, takes the clay from the table to the waste-paper basket, moves to the drinks table, and picks up the matches.* MIDGE HARVEY *enters up centre from left. She is small, neatly dressed but obviously badly off. She is a warm-hearted, practical and very nice young woman, a little younger than* HENRIETTA. *She carries a suitcase.)*

MIDGE. *(as she enters)* Hullo, Cousin Henry.

SIR HENRY. *(turning)* Midge! *(He moves to right of her, takes the suitcase from her, and kisses her.)* Nice to see you.

MIDGE. Nice to see *you.*

SIR HENRY. How are you?

MIDGE. Terribly well.

SIR HENRY. Not been overworking you in that damned dress shop of yours?

MIDGE. *(moving down centre)* Business is pretty slack at the moment, or I shouldn't have got the weekend off. The bus was absolutely crowded; I've never known it go so slowly. *(She sits on the sofa, puts her bag and gloves beside her and looks towards the window right.)* It's heaven to be here. Who's coming this weekend?

SIR HENRY. *(putting the suitcase on the floor right of the armchair left right)* Nobody much. The Cristows. You know them, of course.

MIDGE. The Harley Street doctor with a rather dim wife?

SIR HENRY. That's right. Nobody else. Oh yes – *(he strikes a match)* Edward, of course.

MIDGE. *(turning to face* SIR HENRY*; suddenly stricken by the sound of the name)* Edward!

SIR HENRY. *(lighting his pipe)* Quite a job to get Edward away from Ainswick these days.

MIDGE. *(rising)* Ainswick! Lovely, lovely Ainswick! *(She crosses to the fireplace and gazes up at the picture above it.)*

SIR HENRY. *(moving down centre)* Yes, it's a beautiful place.

MIDGE. *(feelingly)* It's the most beautiful place in the world.

SIR HENRY. *(putting the matchbox on the coffee table)* Had some happy times there, eh? *(He eases to right of the armchair left centre.)*

MIDGE. *(turning)* All the happy times I've ever had were there.

(LADY ANGKATELL enters right. She carries a large empty flower-pot.)

LADY ANGKATELL. *(as she enters)* Would you believe it, *(she crosses above the sofa to right of SIR HENRY)* they've been at it again. They've pushed up a whole row of lovely little lobelias. Ah well, as long as the weather keeps fine…

SIR HENRY. Here's Midge.

LADY ANGKATELL. Where? *(She crosses to MIDGE and kisses her.)* Oh, darling Midge, I didn't see you, dear. *(to SIR HENRY confidentially)* That would help, wouldn't it? What were you both doing when I came in?

SIR HENRY. Talking Ainswick.

LADY ANGKATELL. *(sitting in the armchair left centre; with a sudden change of manner)* Ainswick!

SIR HENRY. *(patting LADY ANGKATELL's shoulder)* There, there, Lucy.

(A little disturbed, he crosses and exits left.)

MIDGE. *(indicating the flower-pot; surprised)* Now why did you bring that in here, darling?

LADY ANGKATELL. I can't begin to think. Take it away.

(MIDGE takes the flower-pot from LADY ANGKATELL, crosses, goes on to the terrace up centre and puts the flower-pot on the ground out of sight.)

Thank you, darling. As I was saying, at any rate the weather's all right. That's *something.* Because if a lot of discordant personalities are boxed up indoors... *(She looks around.)* Where are you?

*(**MIDGE** moves to right of the armchair left centre.)*

Ah, there you are. It makes things ten times worse. Don't you agree?

MIDGE. Makes what worse?

LADY ANGKATELL. One can play games, of course – but that would be like last year when I shall never forgive myself about poor Gerda – and the worst of it is that she really is so nice. It's odd that anyone as nice as Gerda should be so devoid of any kind of intelligence. If that is what they mean by the law of compensation I don't think it's at all fair.

MIDGE. What are you talking about, Lucy?

LADY ANGKATELL. This weekend, darling. *(She takes hold of **MIDGE**'s left hand.)* It's such a relief to talk it over with you, Midge dear, you're so practical.

MIDGE. Yes, but what *are* we talking over?

LADY ANGKATELL. John, of course, is delightful, with that dynamic personality that all really successful doctors seem to have. But as for Gerda, ah well, we must all be very, very kind.

MIDGE. *(crossing to the fireplace)* Come now, Gerda Cristow isn't as bad as all that.

LADY ANGKATELL. Darling. Those eyes. Like a puzzled cow. And she never seems to understand a word one says to her.

MIDGE. I don't suppose she understands a word *you* say – and I don't know that I blame her. Your mind goes so fast, Lucy, that to keep pace with it, your conversation has to take the most astonishing leaps – with all the connecting links left out. *(She sits on the pouffe.)*

LADY ANGKATELL. Like monkeys. Fortunately Henrietta is here. She was wonderful last spring when we played limericks or anagrams – one of those things – we had all finished when we suddenly discovered that poor

Gerda hadn't even started. She didn't even know what the game *was*. It was dreadful, wasn't it, Midge?

MIDGE. Why anyone ever comes to stay with the Angkatells, I don't know. What with the brainwork and the round games and your peculiar style of conversation, Lucy.

LADY ANGKATELL. I suppose we must be rather trying. *(She rises, moves to the coffee table and picks up the tobacco jar.)* The poor dear looked so bewildered; and John looked so impatient. *(She crosses to the fireplace.)* It was then that I was grateful to Henrietta. *(She puts the jar on the mantelpiece, turns and moves centre.)* She turned to Gerda and asked for the pattern of the knitted pullover she was wearing – a dreadful affair in pea green – with little bobbles and pom-poms and things – oh, sordid – but Gerda brightened up at once and looked so pleased. The worst of it is Henrietta had to buy some wool and knit one.

MIDGE. And was it very terrible?

LADY ANGKATELL. Oh, it was ghastly. No – on Henrietta it looked quite charming – which is what I mean when I say that the world is so very very sad. One simply doesn't know *why...*

MIDGE. Woah! Don't start rambling again, darling. Let's stick to the weekend.

(LADY ANGKATELL *sits on the sofa.*)

I don't see where the worry is. If you manage to keep off round games, and try to be coherent when you're talking to Gerda, and put Henrietta on duty to tide over the awkward moments, where's the difficulty?

LADY ANGKATELL. It would all be perfectly all right if only Edward weren't coming.

MIDGE. *(reacting at the name)* Edward? *(She rises and turns to the fireplace.)* Yes, of course. What on earth made you ask Edward for the weekend, Lucy?

LADY ANGKATELL. I didn't ask him. He wired to know if we could have him. You know how sensitive Edward

is. If I'd wired back "No," he would never have asked
himself again. Edward's like that.

MIDGE. Yes.

LADY ANGKATELL. Dear Edward. If only Henrietta would
make up her mind to marry him.

(MIDGE *turns and faces* LADY ANGKATELL.)

She really is quite fond of him. If only they could have
been alone this weekend without the Cristows. As it is,
John has the most unfortunate effect on Edward. John
becomes so much *more* so, and Edward so much *less* so.
If you know what I mean.

(MIDGE *nods.*)

But I do feel that it's all going to be terribly difficult.
(She picks up the "Daily Graphic.")

(GUDGEON, *the butler, enters left He is in all respects
the perfect butler.)*

GUDGEON. *(announcing)* Mr. Edward.

(EDWARD ANGKATELL *enters left. He is a tall, slightly
stooping man, between thirty-five and forty-five, with a
pleasant smile and a diffident manner. He is a bookish
man and wears well-cut but rather shabby tweeds.*
GUDGEON *exits left.)*

LADY ANGKATELL. *(rising and crossing to* EDWARD*)* Edward.
(She kisses him.) We were just saying how nice it was of
you to come.

EDWARD. Lucy, Lucy. How nice of you to *let* me come. *(He
turns to* MIDGE. *Pleased and surprised.)* Why – it's little
Midge. *(He talks throughout to* MIDGE *with indulgent
affection as to a child.)* You look very grown up.

MIDGE. *(with slight acidity)* I've been grown up for quite a
few years now.

EDWARD. I suppose you have. I haven't noticed it.

MIDGE. I know.

EDWARD. At Ainswick, you see, time stands still.

(LADY ANGKATELL turns with a brusque movement, puts the newspaper on the coffee table, then moves to the drinks table, picks up the book from it and puts it in the bookshelves over the drinks table.)

I always remember you as you used to be in the holidays when Uncle Hugh was alive. *(He turns to LADY ANGKATELL.)* I wish you'd come more often to Ainswick, Lucy. It's looking so beautiful just now.

LADY ANGKATELL. Is it, darling?

(GUDGEON enters left.)

GUDGEON. Excuse me, m'lady, but Mrs. Medway would like to see you a moment. It's about the savoury for dinner.

LADY ANGKATELL. Chicken livers. *(She crosses to right of GUDGEON.)* Butchers have no conscience about chicken livers. Don't tell me they haven't arrived.

GUDGEON. They have arrived, m'lady, but Mrs. Medway is a little dubious...

(LADY ANGKATELL crosses and exits left. GUDGEON follows her off, closing the door behind him.)

EDWARD. *(taking his cigarette case from his pocket)* I sometimes wonder whether Lucy minds very much about Ainswick.

MIDGE. In what way?

EDWARD. Well, it was her home. *(He takes a cigarette from his case.)*

MIDGE. May I?

EDWARD. *(offering the case to her)* Yes, of course.

(MIDGE takes a cigarette.)

If she'd been born a boy it would have gone to her instead of to me. I wonder if she resents it? *(He replaces the case in his pocket and takes out his lighter.)*

MIDGE. Not in the sense you mean. After all, you're an Angkatell and that's all that matters. The Angkatells stick together. They even marry their cousins.

EDWARD. Yes, but she does care very much about Ainswick.

MIDGE. Oh yes. Lucy cares more about Ainswick than anything in the world. *(She looks up at the picture over the mantelpiece.)* That picture up there is the dominating note of this house. *(She turns to* **EDWARD**.*)* But if you think Lucy resents *you*, you're wrong, Edward.

EDWARD. *(lighting* **MIDGE**'s *cigarette)* I never quite understand Lucy. *(He turns, moves to left of the sofa and lights his own cigarette.)* She's got the most extraordinary charm.

MIDGE. Lucy is the most adorable creature I know – and the most maddening.

*(***HENRIETTA*** enters left and closes the door behind her. She has tidied herself.)*

HENRIETTA. Hullo, Edward.

EDWARD. Henrietta, lovely to see you.

HENRIETTA. *(crossing to left of* **EDWARD***)* How's Ainswick?

EDWARD. It's looking beautiful just now.

HENRIETTA. *(turning to* **MIDGE***)* Hullo, Midge darling. How are you?

EDWARD. *(offering* **HENRIETTA** *a cigarette)* You ought to come, Henrietta.

HENRIETTA. *(taking a cigarette)* Yes, I know I ought – what fun we all had there as children.

*(***LADY ANGKATELL*** enters left. She carries a large lobster on a short length of string.)*

LADY ANGKATELL. *(crossing to right of the coffee table)* Tradespeople are just like gardeners. They take advantage of your not knowing. Don't you agree, Edward? When you want them to mass in big clumps – they start fiddling about with... *(She suddenly becomes conscious of the lobster.)* Now what *is* that?

EDWARD. It looks to me like a lobster.

LADY ANGKATELL. It is a lobster. Where did I get it? How did I come by it?

HENRIETTA. I should think you got it off the kitchen table.

LADY ANGKATELL. *(holding the lobster against the back of the sofa)* Oh I remember. I thought a cushion this colour would look nice here. What do you feel about it?

HENRIETTA. No!

LADY ANGKATELL. No. Well it was just a little thought.

(**GUDGEON** *enters left and crosses to* **LADY ANGKATELL.** *He carries a salver.*)

GUDGEON. *(impassively)* Excuse me, m'lady, Mrs. Medway says, may she have the lobster.

(**LADY ANGKATELL** *puts the lobster on the salver.*)

Thank you, m'lady.

(*He turns, crosses and exits left. They all laugh.*)

LADY ANGKATELL. Gudgeon is wonderful. *(She sits on the sofa.)* He always appears at the right moment.

HENRIETTA. *(aside)* Could I have a light, Midge?

EDWARD. *(moving to* **LADY ANGKATELL** *and offering her a cigarette)* How's the sculpture, Henrietta?

LADY ANGKATELL. You know I don't smoke, dear.

(**MIDGE** *picks up the table lighter from the mantelpiece.*)

HENRIETTA. Getting along. I've finished the big wooden figure for the International Group. Would you like to see it?

EDWARD. Yes.

HENRIETTA. It's concealed in what I believe the house agent who sold Henry this house calls the "breakfast nook."

(**MIDGE** *lights* **HENRIETTA**'s *cigarette then replaces the lighter on the mantelpiece.*)

LADY ANGKATELL. Thank heavens that's something I have *never* had – my breakfast in a nook.

(*They all laugh.* **HENRIETTA** *moves to the alcove up left, draws back the curtain, switches on the light, then moves up centre.* **EDWARD** *leads* **MIDGE** *to the alcove and stands right of her as they both look off left*)

HENRIETTA. It's called The Worshipper.

EDWARD. *(impressed)* That's a very powerful figure. Beautiful graining. What wood is it?

HENRIETTA. Pearwood.

EDWARD. *(slowly)* It's – an uncomfortable sort of thing.

MIDGE. *(nervously)* It's horrible.

EDWARD. That heavy forward slant of the neck and shoulders – the submission. The fanaticism of the face – the eyes – she's blind? *(He turns to face **HENRIETTA**.)*

HENRIETTA. Yes.

EDWARD. What's she looking at – with her blind eyes?

HENRIETTA. *(turning away)* I don't know. Her God, I suppose.

LADY ANGKATELL. *(softly)* Poor Henrietta.

HENRIETTA. *(moving to right of the armchair left centre)* What did you say, Lucy?

*(**EDWARD** crosses to the fireplace and flicks his ash into it.)*

LADY ANGKATELL. *(rising)* Nothing. *(She moves to right of the sofa and glances off right.)* Ah look, chaffinches. Sweet. One ought to look at birds through glasses, on tops of trees, oughtn't one? *(She turns.)* Are there still herons at Ainswick, Edward?

EDWARD. Ah, yes – down by the river.

LADY ANGKATELL. *(softly)* Down by the river – ah dear.

(Her voice fades away as she exits right.)

EDWARD. Why did she say "Poor Henrietta?"

*(**MIDGE** closes the alcove curtain, switches off the light, crosses above the sofa to right of it, then sits on it at the right end.)*

HENRIETTA. Lucy isn't blind.

EDWARD. *(stubbing out his cigarette in the ashtray on the mantelpiece)* Shall we go for a walk, Henrietta? *(He moves left centre.)* I'd like to stretch my legs after that drive.

HENRIETTA. I'd love to. *(She moves to the coffee table and stubs out her cigarette in the ashtray on it.)* I've been modelling most of the day. Coming, Midge?

MIDGE. No, thank you.

(EDWARD moves slowly up centre.)

I'll stay here and help Lucy with the Cristows when they arrive.

EDWARD. *(stopping and turning; sharply)* Cristow? Is he coming?

HENRIETTA. Yes.

EDWARD. I wish I'd known.

HENRIETTA. *(belligerently)* Why?

EDWARD. *(very quietly)* I could have come – some other weekend.

(There is a pause, then HENRIETTA and EDWARD exit up centre to left. MIDGE watches them go, her face revealing her hopeless love for EDWARD. LADY ANGKATELL enters right and moves above the right end of the sofa.)

LADY ANGKATELL. *(whispering)* Have Henrietta and Edward gone for a walk?

MIDGE. Yes.

LADY ANGKATELL. Does Edward know about the Cristows?

MIDGE. Yes.

LADY ANGKATELL. Was it all right?

MIDGE. Not noticeably.

LADY ANGKATELL. *(moving to the French windows right)* Oh dear. I knew this weekend was going to be awkward.

(MIDGE rises, stubs out her cigarette in the ashtray on the coffee table, picks up her handbag and gloves and moves to LADY ANGKATELL.)

MIDGE. Let's go round the garden, Lucy. What's on in the flower world at the moment? I'm such a hopeless cockney nowadays. Mostly dahlias?

LADY ANGKATELL. Yes. Handsome – in a rather dull way. And so full of earwigs. Mind you, I'm told earwigs are very good mothers, not that it makes one *like* them any better.

(*LADY ANGKATELL and* MIDGE *exit right.* DORIS, *the maid, enters left and holds the door open. She looks slightly half-witted and is terrified of* GUDGEON. GUDGEON *enters left and crosses to the drinks table. He carries a tray of drinks, a bowl of olives and a tea-cloth.* DORIS *closes the door, moves left centre and stands gaping.*)

GUDGEON. (*putting the tray on the drinks table*) Well, fold the papers, Doris, the way I showed you. (*He starts to polish the glasses.*)

DORIS. (*moving hastily to left of the coffee table*) Yes, Mr. Gudgeon. (*She picks up "The Times" and folds it.*) Her ladyship is bats, isn't she, Mr. Gudgeon?

GUDGEON. (*turning*) Certainly not. Her ladyship has a very keen intellect. She speaks five foreign languages, and has been all over the world with Sir Henry. Sir Henry was governor of one of the principal provinces in India. He would have been the next Viceroy most probably if it hadn't been for that terrible Labour government doing away with the empire.

DORIS. (*putting the newspaper on the left arm of the sofa*) My dad's Labour.

(*There is a pause as* GUDGEON *looks almost pityingly at* DORIS.)

(*She takes a step back. Apologetically*) Oh, I'm sorry, Mr. Gudgeon.

GUDGEON. (*tolerantly*) You can't help your parents, Doris.

DORIS. (*humbly*) I know they're not class.

GUDGEON. (*patronizingly*) You are coming along quite nicely – (*he turns to the drinks table and continues polishing the glasses*) – although it's not what any of us have been used to. Gamekeeper's daughter, or Head Groom's daughter, a young girl who knows her manners, and has been brought up right.

(**DORIS** *picks up the "Daily Graphic" and folds it.*)

That's what I like to train.

DORIS. *(putting all the papers together tidily on the coffee table)* Sorry, Mr. Gudgeon. *(She crosses to the writing table, picks up the ashtray from it, returns to the coffee table and empties the ashtray she is carrying into that on the coffee table.)*

GUDGEON. Ah well, it seems those days are gone for ever.

DORIS. *(replacing the ashtray on the writing table)* Miss Simmonds is always down on me, too.

GUDGEON. She's doing it for your own good, Doris. She's training you.

DORIS. *(picking up the ashtray from the coffee table, crossing to the fireplace and emptying the ashtray into the one on the mantelpiece)* Shan't get more money, shall I, when I'm trained?

(She replaces the ashtray on the coffee table.)

GUDGEON. Not much, I'm afraid.

DORIS. *(crossing to the fireplace)* Doesn't seem worth being trained then, does it? *(She picks up the full ashtray from the mantelpiece.)*

GUDGEON. I'm afraid you may be right, my girl.

(**DORIS** *is about to empty the ashtray into the fire.*)

Ah!

(**DORIS** *turns guiltily, and puts the ashtray on the mantelpiece.*)

The trouble is there are no proper *employers* nowadays. Nobody who knows what's what. Those who have the money to employ servants don't appreciate what a good servant is.

DORIS. *(moving to the armchair left centre)* My dad says I ought to call myself a domestic help. *(She tidies the cushion on the armchair.)*

GUDGEON. *(moving above the sofa)* That's about all you are. *(He leans over the back of the sofa and tidies the cushions.)* Let me tell you, my girl, you're very lucky to be in a household where wine glasses are used in the proper way, and where the master and mistress appreciate highly technical skill. *(He moves to the chair down right and tidies the cushion.)* There aren't many employers left who'd even notice if you went the wrong way round the table.

DORIS. *(moving to the fireplace)* I still think her ladyship does funny things. *(She picks up the full ashtray from the mantelpiece.)* Picking up that lobster now.

GUDGEON. *(crossing below the sofa to right of the armchair left centre)* Her ladyship is somewhat forgetful, not to say absent-minded, but in this house I see to it that everything possible is done to spare her ladyship trouble and annoyance.

(The sound of a motor-car horn is heard off.)

(He crosses to the drinks table, picks up the tea-cloth, then crosses to left centre and picks up MIDGE's *suitcase.)* That will be Dr. and Mrs. Cristow. Go upstairs and be ready to help Simmonds with the unpacking.

DORIS. *(moving to the door left and opening it)* Yes, Mr. Gudgeon. *(She starts to exit.)*

GUDGEON. *(reprovingly)* Ah-ah!

DORIS. *(with a step back)* Oh! *(She holds the door open.)*

GUDGEON. *(crossing to the door left)* Thank you.

(A clock strikes seven. He exits left. DORIS *follows him off, leaving the door open.)*

(after the fourth stroke, off left) Good evening, sir.

JOHN. *(off left)* Good evening, Gudgeon. How are you?

GUDGEON. *(off left)* Good evening, madam. Very well, thank you, sir.

GERDA. *(off left)* Good evening, Gudgeon.

(**GUDGEON** *enters left and ushers in* **JOHN** *and* **GERDA CRISTOW.** **JOHN** *is a good-looking man of thirty-eight with a dynamic personality, but is somewhat brusque in manner.* **GERDA** *is timid and rather stupid. She carries an arty leather handbag.*)

GUDGEON. *(as he enters)* Will you come through, madam.

GERDA. *(crossing to left centre)* Very warm, still.

GUDGEON. Still very warm, madam. I hope you had a pleasant drive down.

(**JOHN** *crosses to centre.*)

GERDA. Yes, thank you.

GUDGEON. *(closing the door)* I think her ladyship is in the garden, sir. *(He crosses to right.)* I'll inform her that you've arrived.

JOHN. Thank you, Gudgeon.

(**GUDGEON** *exits right.*)

(*He goes out on to the terrace up centre and looks off left.*) Mm, wonderful to get out of town into this.

GERDA. *(easing to right of the armchair left centre; flatly)* Yes, it's very nice.

JOHN. God, I hate being penned up in London. Sitting in that blasted consulting room, listening to whining women. How I hate sick people!

GERDA. Oh, John, you don't mean that.

JOHN. I loathe illness.

GERDA. If you hated sick people, you wouldn't be a doctor, would you, dear?

JOHN. *(moving above the sofa)* A man doesn't become a doctor because he has a partiality for sick people. It's the disease that's interesting, not the patient. *(He crosses to right and studies the piece of sculpture on the pedestal.)* You have odd ideas, Gerda.

GERDA. But you do like curing people.

JOHN. *(turning)* I don't cure them. *(He moves and sits on the sofa at the right end.)* Just hand out faith, hope and probably a laxative. Oh, good Lord, I'm tired.

GERDA. *(moving below the sofa)* John, you work too hard. You're so unselfish. *(She sits on the sofa at the left end of it.)* I'm always telling the children how a doctor's life is almost a dedication. I'm so proud of the way you give all your time and all your energy and never spare yourself.

JOHN. Oh, for heaven's sake, Gerda. You don't know in the least what you're talking about. Don't you realize I enjoy my profession? It's damned interesting and I make a lot of money.

GERDA. It's not the money you do it for, dear. Look how interested you are in your hospital work. It's to relieve pain and suffering.

JOHN. Pain is a biological necessity and suffering will alway be with us. It's the techniques of medicine that interest me.

GERDA. And – people suffering.

JOHN. *(rising and moving above the sofa)* Oh, for God's sake… *(He breaks off, suddenly ashamed.)* I'm sorry, Gerda. I didn't mean to shout at you. *(He takes a cigarette case from his pocket.)* I'm afraid I've been terribly nervy and bad-tempered lately. I'm – I'm sorry.

GERDA. It's quite all right, dear. *I* understand.

(There is a pause as **JOHN** *moves below the armchair left centre and takes a cigarette out of his case.)*

JOHN. You know, Gerda, if you weren't so patient, so long-suffering, it would be better. Why don't you turn on me sometimes, swear at me, give as good as you get? Oh, don't look so shocked. It would be better if you did. No man likes being drowned in treacle. *(He shuts his cigarette case with a snap and replaces it in his pocket.)*

GERDA. You're tired, John.

JOHN. *(sitting in the armchair left centre; sombrely)* Yes, I'm tired. *(He leans back and closes his eyes.)*

GERDA. You need a holiday.

JOHN. *(dreamily)* I'd like to go to the South of France – the Mediterranean – the sun, the mimosa in flower…

GERDA. *(rising and crossing to right of* JOHN*)* Why shouldn't we go, then? *(doubtfully)* Oh, I don't quite know how we should manage about the children; of course, Terence is at school all day, but he's so rude to Mademoiselle. She really has very little authority even over Zena. No, I don't think I should be very happy. Of course, they could go to Elsie at Bexhill. Or perhaps Mary Foley would take them…

JOHN. *(opening his eyes; vaguely)* 'M, what were you saying?

GERDA. The children.

JOHN. What about them?

GERDA. I was wondering how we could manage about them if we went to the South of France.

JOHN. *(taking his lighter from his pocket)* Why should we go to the South of France, what are you talking about? *(He lights his cigarette.)*

GERDA. Because you said – you – would – like to.

JOHN. Oh that! I was day-dreaming.

GERDA. *(crossing above the armchair left centre to left of it)* I don't see why we couldn't manage it – only it's a little worrying if one feels that the person left in charge isn't really reliable, and I do sometimes feel…

JOHN. *(rising and crossing below the sofa to right)* You never stop worrying about something or other. For heaven's sake let's relax and enjoy this weekend. At least you have a respite from domestic bothers.

GERDA. Yes, I know.

JOHN. *(moving above the sofa)* Wonderful people – the Angkatells. I always find them an absolute tonic.

GERDA. Yes.

JOHN. *(moving on to the terrace up centre)* I wonder where they all are? *(He glances off left.)*

GERDA. *(sitting in the armchair left centre)* Will Henrietta be here?

JOHN. *(turning)* Yes, she's here.

GERDA. Oh, I'm so glad. I do like Henrietta.

JOHN. *(rather shortly)* Henrietta's all right.

GERDA. I wonder if she's finished that statuette she was doing of me?

JOHN. *(moving above the left end of the sofa; sharply)* I don't know why she asked you to sit for her. Most extraordinary.

(GERDA flinches at his tone and look.)

(He crosses to right.) I always think it's rather a good thing if people are around to meet their guests.

(He exits right. GERDA rises, crosses below the sofa to right, looks off, turns, looks left, hesitates, fidgets with her handbag, then gives a nervous cough and crosses to left centre.)

EDWARD. *(off up centre)* And this winter I'm going to cut down that avenue of trees so that we can have a better view of the lake.

(HENRIETTA and EDWARD enter up centre from left. GERDA turns. EDWARD eases to left of the sofa.)

HENRIETTA. *(as she enters)* I think it's a very good idea, Edward. Hullo, Gerda, how are you? You know Edward Angkatell, don't you? *(She eases above the right end of the sofa.)*

EDWARD. How d'you do, Mrs. Cristow?

GERDA. How do you do? *(She drops one glove and picks it up.)*

(EDWARD bends to pick up the glove but GERDA forestalls him.)

HENRIETTA. Where's John?

(EDWARD turns and looks at HENRIETTA.)

GERDA. He just went out into the garden to see if he could find Lady Angkatell.

HENRIETTA. *(moving to the French window right and glancing off)* It's an impossible garden to find anyone in, all woods and shrubs.

GERDA. But soon there'll be such lovely autumn tints.

HENRIETTA. *(turning)* Yes. *(She turns and gazes out of the window.)*

EDWARD. *(crossing to the door left)* You'll forgive me if I go and change.

(He exits left. GERDA starts to follow him but stops as HENRIETTA speaks.)

HENRIETTA. Autumn takes one back – one keeps saying, "Don't you remember?"

(GERDA, strung up and obviously miserable, moves to the armchair left centre.)

(She turns suddenly, looks at GERDA and her face softens.) Shall *we* go and look for the others, too?

GERDA. *(about to sit in the armchair)* No, please – I mean – *(she rises)* yes, that would be very nice.

HENRIETTA. *(moving below the sofa; vigorously)* Gerda! Why do you come down here when you hate it so much?

GERDA. But I don't.

HENRIETTA. *(kneeling with one knee on the sofa)* Yes, you do.

GERDA. I don't really. It's delightful to get down here into the country and Lady Angkatell is always so kind.

HENRIETTA. Lucy? *(She sits on the sofa at the right end of it.)* Lucy's not a bit kind. She has good manners and she knows how to be gracious. But I always think she's rather a cruel person, perhaps because she isn't quite human. She doesn't know what it is to feel and think like ordinary people. And you *are* hating it here, Gerda, you know you are.

GERDA. *(easing to left of the sofa)* Well, you see, John likes it.

HENRIETTA. Oh, John likes it all right. But you could let him come by himself.

GERDA. He wouldn't do that. He wouldn't enjoy himself here without me. He is so unselfish. He thinks it does me good to get down into the country. *(She moves below the left end of the sofa.)* But I'm glad you're here though – it makes it so much better.

HENRIETTA. Does it? I'm glad.

GERDA. *(sitting on the sofa at the left end of it; in a burst of confidence)* You see, I don't really like being away from home. There is so much to do before I leave, and John is so impatient. Even now I'm not sure I turned the bathroom taps off properly, and there was a note I meant to leave for the laundry. And you know, Henrietta, I don't really trust the children's French governess – when I'm not there they never do anything she tells them. Oh well, it's only for two days.

HENRIETTA. Two days of hell – cheerfully endured for John's sake.

GERDA. You must think I'm very ungrateful – when everybody is so kind. My breakfast brought up to my room and the housemaids so beautifully trained – but I do sometimes feel...

HENRIETTA. I know. They snatch away one's clothes and put them where you can't find them, and always lay out the dress and shoes you don't want to wear. One has to be strong-minded.

GERDA. Oh, I'm afraid I'm never strong-minded.

HENRIETTA. How's the knitting?

GERDA. I've taken up leathercraft. *(She holds up her handbag.)* I made this handbag.

HENRIETTA. Did you? *(She rises, crosses to the alcove and opens the curtains.)* That reminds me, I've something for you.

(She switches on the light and exits. She re-enters immediately carrying a small plaster statuette. She switches off the alcove light, closes the curtain and moves to the armchair left centre.)

GERDA. *(rising and crossing to* **HENRIETTA***)* Henrietta! The statuette you were doing of me?

*(***HENRIETTA** *gives* **GERDA** *the statuette.)*

Oh, it's lovely.

HENRIETTA. I'm glad you like it.

GERDA. *(moving below the left end of the sofa)* I do, I like it very much.

JOHN. *(off right)* I say, Sir Henry, your gardener has really made a wonderful job of those roses.

*(***LADY ANGKATELL, JOHN, MIDGE** *and* **SIR HENRY** *enter right.)*

SIR HENRY. *(as he enters)* The soil here is pretty good for roses.

JOHN. *(crossing above the sofa to left of it)* Hello, Henrietta.

HENRIETTA. Hello, John.

LADY ANGKATELL. *(moving below the sofa)* How very nice to see you, Gerda.

SIR HENRY. *(moving above the sofa)* How are you, Mrs. Cristow?

LADY ANGKATELL. *(to* **GERDA***)* You haven't been here for so long. You know my cousin, Midge Harvey? *(She sits on the sofa.)*

MIDGE. *(moving to the writing table)* Yes, we met last year. *(She puts her bag on the writing table.)*

*(***HENRIETTA** *moves to the fireplace, takes a cigarette from the box on the mantelpiece and lights it with the table lighter.)*

GERDA. *(turning and moving to right of* **JOHN***)* John, look what Henrietta's just given me. *(She hands the statuette to him.)*

JOHN. *(to* **HENRIETTA***)* Why – what on earth made you do this?

GERDA. Oh, John, it's very pretty.

JOHN. *(crossing down left, turning and facing* **HENRIETTA***)* Really, Henrietta.

SIR HENRY. *(tactfully interposing)* Mrs. Cristow, I must tell you about our latest excitement. You know the cottage at the end of this lane? It's been taken by a well-known film star, and all the locals are simply goggling.

GERDA. Oh yes, of course – they will be.

MIDGE. Is she very glamorous?

SIR HENRY. Well, I haven't seen her yet, though I believe she's in residence. What's her name now?

MIDGE. Hedy Lamarr?

SIR HENRY. No. Who's that girl with her hair over her eyes?

MIDGE. Veronica Lake.

SIR HENRY. No.

MIDGE. Lauren Bacall.

SIR HENRY. No.

LADY ANGKATELL. Nazimova – no. We'd better ask Gudgeon. He'll know.

SIR HENRY. We saw her in that film – you remember, that tough chap – plays gangsters, and they flew to the Pacific and then flew back again, and there was a particularly horrible child...

MIDGE. *San Francisco Story?*

SIR HENRY. Yes.

MIDGE. Veronica Craye.

*(*JOHN *drops the statuette.* GERDA *moves quickly down left with a cry and picks up the statuette. It is not broken.)*

HENRIETTA. John! *(She watches him with sharpened interest.)*

GERDA. ⎫   ⎧ Oh, John, my statuette.
JOHN.   ⎬ *(together).* ⎨ I'm sorry.
SIR HENRY. ⎭   ⎩ That's it. Blonde with a husky voice.

LADY ANGKATELL. *(rising and crossing to right of* GERDA*)* Would you like to see your room, Gerda?

GERDA. Oh – yes, perhaps I'd better go and unpack.

LADY ANGKATELL. *(crossing below* **GERDA** *to the door left)* Simmonds will have done that. But if you'd like to come up…?

MIDGE. *(crossing to left)* I'll come with you. Where am I, Lucy? In the Blue Room?

LADY ANGKATELL. Yes, and I've put Edward in the Hermit, and I've put the rest…

(Her voice dies away as she exits left. **GERDA** *and* **MIDGE** *follow her off.* **JOHN** *stands in a daze.)*

SIR HENRY. Where is Edward? Has he put his car away, I wonder? There's room in the end garage.

(He exits up centre to left. **HENRIETTA** *moves to* **JOHN** *and gives him her cigarette. Now that they are alone her voice holds a new intimacy.)*

HENRIETTA. Is anything the matter, darling?

JOHN. *(crossing to the sofa)* M'm? I was – thinking – remembering. I'm sorry. *(He sits on the sofa at the left end, and faces right.)*

HENRIETTA. *(easing to the fireplace)* There's an atmosphere of remembering about this place. *(She turns and looks at the picture over the mantelpiece.)* I've been remembering, too.

JOHN. Have you? *(disinterested)* Remembering what?

HENRIETTA. *(turning; bitterly)* The time when I was a long-legged lanky girl with untidy hair – a happy girl with no idea of the things that life could do to her. *(She turns to face the fire.)* Going back…

JOHN. *(dreamily)* Why should one want to go back – suddenly? Why do things you haven't thought of for years suddenly spring into your mind?

HENRIETTA. *(turning)* What things, John?

JOHN. *(dreamily)* Blue sea – the smell of mimosa…

HENRIETTA. When?

JOHN. Ten years ago.

HENRIETTA. *(crossing to left of the sofa)* And you'd like – to go back?

JOHN. I don't know – I'm so tired.

(HENRIETTA, from behind, lays a hand on JOHN's shoulder.)

(He holds her hand but still stares dreamily right.) What would I do without you?

HENRIETTA. Get along quite well, I expect.

JOHN. Why should things come back into your mind – things that are over and done with?

HENRIETTA. *(crossing above the sofa to right of it)* Perhaps because they are *not* really over and done with.

JOHN. Not after ten years? Heaven knows how long since I thought about it. But lately – even when I'm walking round the wards, it comes into my mind and it's as vivid as a picture. *(He pauses. With sudden energy)* And now, on top of it all, she's here, just a few yards down the lane.

HENRIETTA. *(moving below the right end of the sofa)* Veronica Craye, you mean?

JOHN. Yes. I was engaged to her once – ten years ago.

HENRIETTA. *(sitting on the sofa at the right end of it)* I – see.

JOHN. Crazy young fool! I was mad about her. She was just starting in pictures then. I'd qualified about a year before. I'd had a wonderful chance – to work under Radley. D. H. Radley, you know, *the* authority on cortex degeneration.

HENRIETTA. What happened?

JOHN. What I might have guessed would happen. Veronica got her chance to go to Hollywood. Well, naturally, she took it. But she assumed, without making any bones about it, that I'd give up everything and go with her. *(He laughs.)* No idea how important my profession was to me. I can hear her now. "Oh, there's absolutely no need for you to go on doctoring – *I* shall be making heaps of money." *(He gives his cigarette to HENRIETTA.)* I tried to explain it all to her. Radley – what a wonderful opportunity it was to work under him. Do you know what she said? "What, that comic little old man?" I told her that that comic little old man had done some of the most remarkable work of our generation – that his experiments might revolutionize the treatment of Rigg's Disease. But of course that was a waste of time. She'd never even heard of Rigg's Disease.

HENRIETTA. Very few people have. I hadn't till you told me about it and I read it up.

(JOHN rises, moves up centre, goes on to the terrace and stands facing left.)

JOHN. She said who cared about a lot of obscure diseases anyway. California was a wonderful climate – it would be fun for me to see the world. She'd hate to go there without me. Miss Craye was the complete egoist – never thought of anyone but herself.

HENRIETTA. You're rather by way of being an egoist too, John.

JOHN. *(turning to face* HENRIETTA*)* I saw her point of view. Why couldn't she see mine?

HENRIETTA. What did you suggest?

JOHN. *(moving to the sofa and leaning over the back of it)* I told her I loved her. I begged her to turn down the Hollywood offer and marry me there and then.

HENRIETTA. And what did she say to that?

JOHN. *(bitterly)* She was just – amused.

HENRIETTA. And so?

JOHN. *(moving down right)* Well, there was only one thing to be done – break it off. I did. It wasn't easy. All that was when we were in the South of France. *(He crosses to the coffee table, picks up a magazine, then crosses and stands below the armchair left centre.)* I broke with Veronica, and came back to London to work under Radley. *(During the following speeches he occasionally glances idly at the magazine.)*

HENRIETTA. And then you married Gerda?

JOHN. The following year. Yes.

HENRIETTA. Why?

JOHN. *Why?*

HENRIETTA. Yes. Was it because you wanted someone as different as possible from Veronica Craye?

JOHN. Yes, I suppose that was it. *(He sits in the armchair left centre.)* I didn't want a raving beauty as a wife. I didn't want a damned egoist out to grab everything she could get. I wanted safety and peace and devotion, and all the quiet enduring things of life. I wanted someone who'd take her ideas from *me*.

HENRIETTA. Well, you certainly got what you wanted. No-one could be more devoted to you than Gerda.

JOHN. That's the irony of it. I picked Gerda for just the qualities she has, and now half the time I snap her head off because of them. How was I to know how irritating devotion can be?

HENRIETTA. *(rising and stubbing out her cigarette in the ashtray on the coffee table)* And what about Gerda? Is she satisfied?

JOHN. Oh, Gerda's all right. She's quite happy.

HENRIETTA. Is she?

JOHN. Oh, yes. She spends her life fussing about the house and the children. That's all she thinks about. She's the most incompetent housekeeper and the most injudicious mother that you can imagine. Still, it keeps her occupied.

HENRIETTA. *(crossing to right of* **JOHN***)* How horribly cruel you are, John.

JOHN. *(surprised)* Me?

HENRIETTA. Do you never see or feel anything except from your own point of view? Why do you bring Gerda down here for weekends when you know it's misery for her?

JOHN. Nonsense! Does her a world of good to get away. It makes a break for her.

HENRIETTA. Sometimes, John, I really hate you.

JOHN. *(startled)* Henrietta. *(He rises.)* Darling – don't say that. You know it's only you who make life possible for me.

HENRIETTA. I wonder. *(She puts up a hand to touch him lovingly, then checks herself.)*

(JOHN kisses her, then crosses and puts the magazine on the coffee table.)

JOHN. Who's the Edward Angkatell?

HENRIETTA. A second cousin of mine – and of Henry's.

JOHN. Have I met him?

HENRIETTA. Twice.

JOHN. I don't remember. *(He perches himself on the left arm of the sofa.)* Is he in love with you, Henrietta?

HENRIETTA. Yes.

JOHN. Well, you watch your step. You're mine, you know.

(HENRIETTA looks at him in silence.)

And look here, what do you mean by doing that absurd statuette of Gerda? Hardly up to your standard, is it?

HENRIETTA. It's technically quite good craftsmanship – a straightforward portrait statuette. It pleased Gerda.

JOHN. Oh, Gerda!

HENRIETTA. It was made to please her.

JOHN. Gerda doesn't know the difference between a work of art and a coloured photograph. What about your pearwood figure for the International Group? Have you finished that?

HENRIETTA. Yes.

JOHN. Let's have a look at it.

(HENRIETTA moves unwillingly to the alcove, opens the curtain, switches on the light, then stands left of the arch and watches JOHN's face. JOHN rises, crosses to the alcove and stands in the arch looking off left.)

I say, that's rather good. Why, what on earth…? *(angrily)* So *that's* why you wanted Gerda to sit for you. How dare you!

HENRIETTA. *(thoughtfully)* I wondered if you'd see it.

JOHN. See it? Of course I see it.

HENRIETTA. The face isn't Gerda's.

JOHN. No, it's the neck – the shoulders – the whole attitude.

(The daylight starts to fade and continues to do so steadily until the end of the Act.)

HENRIETTA. Yes, that's what I wanted.

JOHN. *How could you do a thing like that?* It's indefensible.

HENRIETTA. You don't understand, John. You don't know what it is to want something – to look at it day after day – that line of neck – the muscle – the angle of the head – that heaviness under the jaw. I've been looking at them, wanting them, every time I saw Gerda. In the end – I just had to have them.

JOHN. Utterly unscrupulous.

HENRIETTA. Yes – I suppose you could call it that.

JOHN. *(uneasily)* That's a terrifying thing you've made, Henrietta. What's she looking at – who is it there, in front of her?

HENRIETTA. I don't know, John. I think – it might be *you.*

*(**EDWARD** enters left. He now wears dinner clothes.)*

You remember Edward – John.

JOHN. *(tersely)* Of course.

EDWARD. *(moving below the armchair left centre)* Looking at Henrietta's latest masterpiece?

JOHN. *(without looking at **EDWARD**)* Yes. *(He crosses to the fireplace.)* Yes, I was.

EDWARD. What do you think of it?

JOHN. *(with his back to **EDWARD**)* I'm not really qualified to judge. *(He takes a cigarette from his case.)*

EDWARD. Powerful!

JOHN. 'M?

EDWARD. I said it's powerful.

JOHN. Yes.

HENRIETTA. *(switching off the light and closing the alcove curtain)* I must go and change.

EDWARD. Still lots of time. *(He crosses to the drinks table.)* Can I get you a drink, Cristow?

JOHN. No, thank you. *(He taps his cigarette on his case.)*

EDWARD. *(moving to the French window right)* Quite a mild evening.

(He glances at HENRIETTA and JOHN, then exits right.)

HENRIETTA. *(moving centre)* You were very rude, John.

JOHN. *(turning)* I've no time for that sort of person.

HENRIETTA. Edward's a dear.

JOHN. Possibly. *(He lights his cigarette.)* I don't like him. I think he is quite ineffectual.

HENRIETTA. You know, sometimes, John, I'm afraid for you.

JOHN. Afraid for me? What do you mean?

HENRIETTA. It's dangerous to be as oblivious as you are.

JOHN. Oblivious?

HENRIETTA. You never see or know anything that people are feeling about you.

JOHN. I should have said the opposite.

HENRIETTA. You see what you're looking *at* – yes. You're like a searchlight. A powerful beam turned on to the one spot where your interest is, but behind it, and each side of it, darkness.

JOHN. Henrietta, darling, what is all this?

HENRIETTA. I tell you, it's *dangerous*. You assume everybody likes you – *(She moves in to right of JOHN.)* Lucy and Gerda, Henry, Midge and Edward.

(JOHN puts his cigarette in the ashtray on the mantelpiece)

Do you know at all what they feel about you?

JOHN. *(smiling)* And Henrietta? What does she feel? At least –
(he catches her hand and draws her to him) I'm sure of you.

HENRIETTA. You can be sure of no-one in this world, John.

(**JOHN** *kisses her. As she gives in to him helplessly, he
releases her, smiles, turns, picks up his cigarette and
moves to the door left.* **EDWARD** *enters right.* **JOHN** *gives*
EDWARD *a cynical look then exits left.)*

HENRIETTA. *(cont., turning to* **EDWARD.***)* Get me a drink,
would you, Edward, before I go. *(She turns, looks in the
mirror on the mantelpiece and touches up her lipstick with her
handkerchief.)*

EDWARD. *(moving to the drinks table)* Sherry?

HENRIETTA. Please.

EDWARD. *(pouring out two sherries)* I wish you'd come to
Ainswick more often, Henrietta. It's a long time now.

HENRIETTA. I know. One gets tangled up in things.

EDWARD. Is that the real reason?

HENRIETTA. Not quite.

EDWARD. You can tell me, Henrietta.

HENRIETTA. *(turning; feelingly)* You are a dear, Edward. I'm
very fond of you.

EDWARD. *(crossing to right of* **HENRIETTA** *with the drinks)* Why
don't you come to Ainswick? *(He hands a drink to her.)*

HENRIETTA. Because – one can't go back.

EDWARD. You used to be happy there, in the old days.

HENRIETTA. Yes, happy in the loveliest way of all – when
one doesn't know one is happy.

EDWARD. *(raising his glass)* To Ainswick.

HENRIETTA. *(raising her glass)* Ainswick.

(They both laugh, then sip their drinks.)

Is it the same, Edward? Or has it changed? Things do
change.

EDWARD. *I* don't change.

HENRIETTA. No, darling Edward. You're always the same.

EDWARD. Same old stick-in-the-mud.

HENRIETTA. *(crossing below* EDWARD *to the sofa)* Don't say that. *(She sits on the sofa at the left end.)*

EDWARD. It's true. I've never been very good at – doing things.

HENRIETTA. I think perhaps you're wise not to do things.

EDWARD. That's an odd thing for you to say, Henrietta. You who've been so successful.

HENRIETTA. Sculpture isn't a thing you set out to do and succeed in. It's something that gets *at* you – and haunts you – so that, in the end, you just have to make terms with it. And then – for a while – you get some peace.

EDWARD. Do you want to be peaceful, Henrietta?

HENRIETTA. Sometimes I think I want to be peaceful more than anything in the world.

EDWARD. *(crossing to left of the sofa)* You could be peaceful at Ainswick. *(He puts his hand on* HENRIETTA*'s shoulder.)* I think you could be happy there. Even – even if you had to put up with me. *(He crosses and sits on the sofa at the right end of it.)* What about it, Henrietta? Won't you come to Ainswick and make it your home? It's always been there, you know, waiting for you.

HENRIETTA. Edward, I wish I weren't so very fond of you. It makes it so much more difficult to go on saying no.

EDWARD. It is no, then?

HENRIETTA. *(putting her glass on the coffee table)* I'm sorry.

EDWARD. You've said no before, but this time – *(He rises.)* well, I thought it might be different. When we walked in the woods your face was so young and happy, *(He moves to the window right.)* almost as it used to be. Talking about Ainswick, thinking about Ainswick. Don't you see what that means, Henrietta?

HENRIETTA. Edward, we've been living this afternoon in the past.

EDWARD. *(moving to right of the sofa)* The past is sometimes a very good place to live.

HENRIETTA. One can't go back. That's the one thing you can't do – go back.

(There is a pause. **EDWARD** *moves above the sofa to left of it and looks towards the door left.)*

EDWARD. *(quietly)* What you really mean is that you won't marry me because of John Cristow. *(He pauses, then turns.)* That's it, isn't it? If there were no John Cristow in the world you would marry me.

HENRIETTA. I can't imagine a world in which there was no John Cristow.

*(***SIR HENRY*** enters left. He now wears dinner clothes.* **HENRIETTA** *rises.)*

SIR HENRY. *(switching on the wall-bracket and mantelpiece lights by the switch below the fireplace)* Hurry up, Henrietta. It's nearly dinner time.

HENRIETTA. *(crossing to the door left)* I'll be quick as a flash.

(She exits hurriedly left. **EDWARD** *sits on the sofa at the left end of it.)*

SIR HENRY. *(crossing to the drinks table)* Have you got a drink, Edward? *(He switches on the table-lamp on the drinks table.)*

EDWARD. Thank you, yes.

SIR HENRY. *(mixing cocktails)* Haven't seen much of you since Lucy and I settled down at The Hollow.

EDWARD. No. How does it affect you both – laying aside the cares of state?

SIR HENRY. I sometimes think, Edward, that you've been the wisest of the family.

EDWARD. That's an original point of view. I always regard myself as a walking example of how to fail in life.

SIR HENRY. Oh no, it's a question of the right values. To look after one's estate and to read and care for one's books—

*(***MIDGE*** enters left She wears an evening frock.* **EDWARD** *rises.)*

– not to compete in the struggle for material achievement... *(He turns to* **MIDGE.***)* Hullo, there – that's a pretty frock.

MIDGE. *(moving left centre and turning completely around, showing off her frock)* One of my perks from the shop.

EDWARD. You can't really like working in a shop, Midge.

MIDGE. *(crossing to the drinks table)* Who said I like it? *(She picks up the bowl of olives.)*

EDWARD. *(resuming his seat on the sofa)* Then why do it?

MIDGE. What do you suggest I should live on? Beautiful thoughts?

EDWARD. *(shocked)* But, my dear girl, if I'd had any idea you were hard up...

SIR HENRY. Save your breath, Edward. She's obstinate. Refused an allowance and won't come and live with us, though we've begged her to. I can't think of anything nicer than having young Midge about the house.

EDWARD. Why don't you, Midge?

MIDGE. *(moving right of the sofa then below it)* I have ideas. *(She offers the olives to* **EDWARD.***)* Poor, proud and prejudiced –

*(***EDWARD** *shakes his head, refusing the olives.)*

– that's me.

*(***LADY ANGKATELL** *enters left. She wears an evening gown,* **EDWARD** *rises.)*

They're badgering me, Lucy.

LADY ANGKATELL. *(crossing to the armchair left centre)* Are they, darling? *(She sits.)*

EDWARD. I don't like the idea of her working in that dress shop.

MIDGE. *(crossing to* **LADY ANGKATELL***)* Well, find me a better job. *(She offers the olives to her.)*

*(***LADY ANGKATELL** *takes an olive.* **MIDGE** *moves to the fireplace and puts the dish on the mantelpiece.)*

EDWARD. There surely must be something...

MIDGE. I've no particular qualifications, remember. Just a pleasant manner and the ability to keep my temper when I'm shouted at.

EDWARD. Do you mean to say the customers are rude to you?

MIDGE. Abominably rude, sometimes. *(She sits on the pouffe.)* It's their privilege.

EDWARD. *(crossing to the fireplace; horrified)* But, my dear girl, that's all wrong. *(He puts his glass on the mantelpiece.)* If I'd only known... *(He takes his case from his pocket and offers* MIDGE *a cigarette.)*

MIDGE. *(taking a cigarette)* How should you know? Your world and mine are so far apart.

(EDWARD *lights* MIDGE's *cigarette.)*

I'm only half an Angkatell. The other half's just plain business girl, with unemployment always lurking round the corner in spite of the politicians' brave words.

SIR HENRY. *(crossing to* MIDGE *with two drinks)* You be a good girl and drink that. *(He hands one drink to her.)* What's rubbed your fur up the wrong way, kitten? *(He offers the other drink to* LADY ANGKATELL.*)*

LADY ANGKATELL. *(to* SIR HENRY*)* Sherry for me, dear.

(SIR HENRY *moves to the drinks table.)* Edward does have that effect sometimes.

(GERDA *enters left. She wears an evening frock.)*

GERDA. *(crossing to right of* LADY ANGKATELL*)* I'm so sorry if I'm late.

LADY ANGKATELL. *(holding* GERDA's *hand)* But you're not at all late, my dear.

MIDGE. We've just come down.

SIR HENRY. What will you have, Mrs. Cristow – sherry – gin?

(JOHN *enters left. He wears dinner clothes.)*

GERDA. *(crossing to left of the drinks table)* Oh – thank you, gin and something, please.

JOHN. Am I the last? *(He crosses down right.)*

LADY ANGKATELL. Henrietta isn't down yet.

(**SIR HENRY** *crosses with a drink to* **LADY ANGKATELL** *and hands it to her, then returns to the drinks table and pours a drink for* **GERDA**. *The conversations overlap in a hubbub of talk.*)

LADY ANGKATELL. Midge, dear, what a pretty dress.

EDWARD. Yes, it is charming, isn't it?

MIDGE. If you knew the trouble I had getting it.

LADY ANGKATELL. How can you afford it on your salary, dear?

MIDGE. I got it from the shop.

LADY ANGKATELL. The shop?

EDWARD. Yes, it's one of your perks, didn't you say, Midge?

LADY ANGKATELL. Perks? Do you mean to say you get them for nothing? Henry, darling, do you know that this child gets…

SIR HENRY. What will you have, Cristow? Sherry, gin?

JOHN. I'd love some sherry, if I may.

SIR HENRY. There's a very good dry Martini here, but if you'd prefer sherry…

JOHN. Yes, it's wonderful, I know. I'd like some sherry. I remember your dry Martinis from last July.

GERDA. (*crossing to right*). This is very nice.

JOHN. It will go straight to your head, if you are not careful.

(**VERONICA CRAYE** *enters on the terrace up centre from left and stands posed in the French windows. She is a very beautiful woman and knows it. She wears a resplendent evening gown and carries an evening bag. Her appearance causes a sensation.* **JOHN** *stares at her like a man dazed.* **MIDGE** *and* **LADY ANGKATELL** *rise. They all turn and stare at* **VERONICA**.)

VERONICA. (*moving to right of* **LADY ANGKATELL**) You must forgive me – for bursting in upon you this way. I'm your neighbour, Lady Angkatell – from that ridiculous cottage, Dovecotes – and the most awful thing has happened. *(She moves centre and dominates the scene.)* Not a single match in the house and my lighter won't work. So what could I do? I just came along to beg help from my only neighbour within miles.

LADY ANGKATELL. Why, of course. How awkward for you.

VERONICA. *(turning right and affecting to see* JOHN *quite suddenly)* Why, surely – *John!* Why, it's John Cristow. *(She crosses to left of* JOHN *and takes hold of both of his hands.)* Now isn't that amazing? I haven't seen you for years and years and years. And suddenly – to find you – here. This is just the most wonderful surprise. *(To* LADY ANGKATELL.*)* John's an old friend of mine. *(She retains hold of* JOHN*'s left hand.)* Why, John's the first man I ever loved.

SIR HENRY. *(moving above the sofa with two drinks)* Sherry? Or dry Martini?

VERONICA. No, no, thank you.

   *(*JOHN *takes a sherry from* SIR HENRY.*)*

LADY ANGKATELL. *(resuming her seat in the armchair left centre)* Midge dear, ring the bell.

   *(*MIDGE *moves below the fireplace and presses the bell-push.)*

VERONICA. I hope you don't think it's just too awful of me butting in like this.

LADY ANGKATELL. Not at all.

SIR HENRY. *(moving up centre)* We are honoured. *(He indicates* MIDGE.*)* My cousin, Miss Harvey. Edward Angkatell. *(He looks towards* GERDA.*)* Er…

   *(*GERDA *eases down right of* JOHN.*)*

JOHN. And this is my wife, Veronica.

VERONICA. *(crossing below* JOHN *to left of* GERDA *and taking her by the hand)* Oh, but how lovely to meet you.

   *(*GUDGEON *enters left.)*

GUDGEON. You rang, m'lady?

LADY ANGKATELL. A dozen boxes of matches, please, Gudgeon.

(**GUDGEON** *is momentarily taken aback, but regains his normal impassivity immediately and exits left.*)

SIR HENRY. And how do you like living at Dovecotes?

VERONICA. *(turning)* I adore it. *(She crosses upstage to left of the sofa and looks off right.)* I think it's so wonderful to be right in the heart of the country – these lovely English woods – and yet to be quite near London.

SIR HENRY. You've no idea what a thrill you've caused in the neighbourhood. But you must be used to that sort of thing.

VERONICA. Well, I've signed a few autograph books, *(She eases below the left end of the sofa.)* but what I like about it here is that one isn't in a village, and there's no-one to stare or gape. *(She sits on the sofa at the left end.)* I just appreciate the peacefulness of it all.

(**GUDGEON** *enters left. He carries a packet of a dozen boxes of matches on a salver.*)

LADY ANGKATELL. *(indicating **VERONICA**)* For madam.

(**GUDGEON** *crosses to* **VERONICA.**)

VERONICA. *(taking the matches)* Oh dear, Lady Angkatell – I can't really accept…

LADY ANGKATELL. Please. It's nothing at all.

VERONICA. Well, I do appreciate your kindness.

(**GUDGEON** *crosses and exits left.*)

John, do you live in this neighbourhood too?

JOHN. No – no, I live in London. I'm just down here for the weekend.

VERONICA. Oh, I just can't get over meeting you again after all these years.

(**HENRIETTA** *enters left and moves to left of* **LADY ANGKATELL.** *She wears an evening frock.*)

(She glances at **HENRIETTA** *and rises.)* Now – I must get back – carrying my spoils with me. John, will you see me down the lane?

*(***LADY ANGKATELL*** *rises.)*

JOHN. Yes, of course.

VERONICA. *(crossing to right of* **LADY ANGKATELL***)* And thank you a thousand times. *(She smiles at* **SIR HENRY** *and* **EDWARD** *but ignores the ladies.)* You've all been very kind.

*(***JOHN*** *moves to the drinks table and puts his glass on it.)*

LADY ANGKATELL. Not at all.

VERONICA. *(crossing above the sofa to* **JOHN***)* Now, John, you must tell me all you've been doing in the years and years since I've seen you.

*(***GUDGEON*** *enters left.)*

GUDGEON. Dinner is served, m'lady.

(He exits left.)

VERONICA. Oh, I mustn't take you away just as dinner is ready.

SIR HENRY. Won't you stay and dine with us?

VERONICA. No, no, no. I couldn't dream of it. John, can't you come over after dinner? I'm just dying to hear all your news. I'll be expecting you. *(She goes up the steps, turns and stands in the French window up centre)* And thank you all – so much.

(She exits up centre to left. **JOHN** *stands right of the French window up centre and looks after her.* **LADY ANGKATELL** *hands her glass to* **EDWARD***, who puts it on the mantelpiece.* **MIDGE** *puts her glass on the mantelpiece, moves to the door left and opens it.* **JOHN** *goes on to the terrace.)*

LADY ANGKATELL. What a beautiful performance! Shall we go in to dinner? *(She crosses to the door left.)*

(*SIR HENRY crosses to the door left. A hubbub of conversation breaks out and the following speeches overlap as the exits are made.*)

I remember seeing that girl in a film. She was wearing a sari very low down.

(*She exits left.*)

EDWARD. I've seen her too, but I can't remember the name of the film.

MIDGE. *San Francisco Story* – it must be. It was revived about two months ago.

(*She exits left.*)

EDWARD. Which theatre? Did you see *San Francisco Story?*

SIR HENRY. She must have changed her hair. She had it flowing down her back. Mrs. Cristow, what do you think of our film star?

(*GERDA crosses to the door left.*)

GERDA. She's very nice, very nice indeed, really.

(*She exits left.*)

EDWARD. Yes, she is. Isn't she, Henry?

SIR HENRY. Not so tall as I should have thought, seeing her on the films.

(*He exits left.*)

EDWARD. No, I agree, but they are very different in real life.

(*He exits left. The conversation continues offstage. JOHN, oblivious of everything else, stands on the terrace looking off left. HENRIETTA moves to the door left and turns.*)

HENRIETTA. Are you coming, John?

JOHN. H'm? Oh yes – yes, of course.

(*HENRIETTA exits left. JOHN crosses to the door left and follows her off as – the curtain falls*)

ACT TWO

(*Scene – The same. Saturday morning.*)

(*When the curtain rises it is a fine morning. The clock is striking eleven. The French windows are open and music is coming softly from the radio. The tune is "I Cried For You." JOHN enters briskly left. He is humming, looks happy and good-tempered. He moves to left centre, checks his watch with the clock on the mantelpiece, goes on to the terrace up centre, takes a cigarette from his case and lights it. GUDGEON enters left. He carries a salver with a note on it.*)

GUDGEON. (*moving left centre*) A note for you, sir.

JOHN. (*moving to right of GUDGEON; surprised*) For me? (*He takes the note.*)

GUDGEON. They are waiting for an answer, sir.

JOHN. It looks as though it's going to be a fine day, Gudgeon.

GUDGEON. Yes, sir. There was quite a haze over the downs early this morning.

(*JOHN reads the note and frowns angrily.*)

JOHN. There's no answer, Gudgeon.

GUDGEON. (*turning and crossing to the door left*) Very good, sir.

JOHN. Where is everybody?

GUDGEON. (*stopping and turning*) Her ladyship has gone down to the farm, sir. The gentlemen have gone out shooting, and I believe Miss Harvey and Miss Henrietta are in the garden.

JOHN. Thank you, Gudgeon.

(GUDGEON exits left. JOHN moves on to the terrace up centre, re-reads the note, utters an angry ejaculation, crumples the note and puts it in his pocket. MIDGE enters right. She carries an armful of dahlias and loose leaves.)

MIDGE. *(crossing to left of the coffee table)* Good morning. *(She kneels, takes the vase from the coffee table and starts filling it with the dahlias.)*

JOHN. Good morning.

MIDGE. Gerda up yet?

JOHN. No, she had breakfast in bed. She had a headache. I told her to lie in for once.

MIDGE. I meant to spend the whole morning in bed, but it was so lovely outside that I couldn't.

JOHN. Where's Henrietta?

MIDGE. I don't know. She was with me just now. She may be in the rose garden.

(JOHN exits up centre to right. LADY ANGKATELL enters left. She carries a basket of eggs.)

LADY ANGKATELL. Music? *(She moves to the radio.)* Oh no, dear, oh no – no. *(She switches off the radio.)* Stop! We can't be swinging so early in the day.

MIDGE. I wish you'd do these dahlias, Lucy. They defeat me.

LADY ANGKATELL. *(crossing to the drinks table)* Do they, darling? *(She puts the basket on the floor left of the drinks table.)* What a shame – never mind. *(She moves dreamily to the writing table.)* Now then, what did I want? Ah, I know. *(She lifts the telephone receiver.)* Now let me see – ah yes, this thing. *(She cradles the receiver first in one arm and then in the other.)*

(MIDGE stares amazed at LADY ANGKATELL.)

(with satisfaction) Ah! I see what it is. *(She replaces the receiver.)*

MIDGE. What *are* you doing, Lucy?

LADY ANGKATELL. Doing?

MIDGE. You seemed to be having a kind of game with the telephone receiver.

LADY ANGKATELL. Oh, that was Mrs. Bagshaw's baby. *(She looks at* **MIDGE.***)* You've got the wrong vase, darling.

MIDGE. *(rising)* What did you say?

LADY ANGKATELL. I said you'd got the wrong vase. It's the white vase for dahlias.

MIDGE. No, I meant what did you say about somebody's baby?

LADY ANGKATELL. Oh, that was the telephone receiver, my pet.

MIDGE. *(moving to the drinks table)* I don't wonder that Gerda Cristow nearly has a nervous breakdown every time you talk to her. *(She picks up the white vase and jug of water from the drinks table, moves and puts them on the coffee table.)* What has Mrs. Bagshaw's baby got to do with the telephone receiver? *(She pours some water into the vase and fills it with the dahlias, during the ensuing speeches.)*

LADY ANGKATELL. She seemed to be holding it – the baby I mean – upside down. So I was trying this way and that way. And of course I see what it is – she's left-handed. That's why it looked all wrong. Is John Cristow down yet?

MIDGE. Yes, he went into the garden to look for Henrietta.

LADY ANGKATELL. *(sitting on the sofa at the right end of it)* Oh! Do you think that was very wise of him?

MIDGE. What do you mean?

LADY ANGKATELL. Well, I don't want to say anything…

MIDGE. Come on, Lucy. Give.

LADY ANGKATELL. Well, you know, darling, that I don't sleep very well. And when I can't sleep I'm inclined to prowl around the house.

MIDGE. I know, half the guests think it's burglars, the other half think it's ghosts.

LADY ANGKATELL. Well, I happened to be looking through the passage window. John was just coming back to the house, and it was close on three o'clock.

(There is a pause. **MIDGE** *and* **LADY ANGKATELL** *look at each other.)*

MIDGE. *(picking up the jug and vase of dahlias and crossing with them to the drinks table)* Even for old friends who have a lot to say to each other, three in the morning is a little excessive. *(She puts the jug and vase on the drinks table.)* One wonders what Gerda thinks about it.

LADY ANGKATELL. One wonders if Gerda thinks.

MIDGE. *(easing above the sofa)* Even the meekest of wives may turn.

LADY ANGKATELL. I don't think Henrietta was sleeping very well either last night. The light was on in her room, and I thought I saw her curtains move.

MIDGE. Really, John is a *fool.*

LADY ANGKATELL. He's a man who's always taken risks – and usually got away with them.

MIDGE. One day he'll go too far. This was a bit blatant, even for him.

LADY ANGKATELL. My dear child, he couldn't help himself. That woman just sailed in last night and – grabbed him. I must say I admired her performance. It was so beautifully timed and planned.

MIDGE. Do you think it was planned?

LADY ANGKATELL. *(rising)* Well, darling, come, come. *(She smiles, picks up the "Daily Mirror" and crosses to the fireplace.)*

MIDGE. You may say, in your detached way, she gave a beautiful performance – but it remains to be seen whether Gerda and Henrietta agree with you.

*(***SIR HENRY*** enters left. He carries two revolvers.)*

SIR HENRY. *(crossing to right)* Just going to have a little practice down at the targets. Like to come along and try your hand, Midge?

MIDGE. I've never shot with a pistol or a revolver in my life. I shall probably drill a hole in you, Cousin Henry.

SIR HENRY. I'll take jolly good care that you don't.

MIDGE. Well, it would be nice to think that I might some day be able to turn the tables on a burglar.

SIR HENRY. Every woman ought to learn to shoot with a revolver.

LADY ANGKATELL. *(moving and sitting in the armchair left centre)* Now you're on Henry's hobby. He has a whole collection of pistols and revolvers, including a lovely pair of French duelling pistols. *(She starts to read the paper.)*

MIDGE. Don't you have to have licences for them?

SIR HENRY. Of course.

MIDGE. Have you ever had a burglar?

SIR HENRY. Not yet, but we live in hopes. If he does come, Lucy will probably shoot him dead.

MIDGE. *(surprised),* Lucy?

SIR HENRY. Lucy's a far better shot than I am. Lucy always gets her man.

MIDGE. I shall be simply terrified.

(She exits right. SIR HENRY follows her off. HENRIETTA enters up centre from left.)

HENRIETTA. *(easing above the sofa)* Hullo, are the Angkatells going to exterminate each other?

LADY ANGKATELL. They've gone down to the targets. Why don't you join them, Henrietta?

HENRIETTA. Yes, I will. I was rather good last spring. Are you going, Lucy?

LADY ANGKATELL. Yes. No. I must do something about my eggs first. *(She looks around.)*

HENRIETTA. Eggs?

LADY ANGKATELL. Yes, they are over there in the basket, darling.

(**HENRIETTA** *moves to the drinks table, picks up the basket of eggs and takes it to* **LADY ANGKATELL**.)

Oh! Thank you, my pet. *(She puts the basket on the floor right of her chair, then resumes reading.)*

HENRIETTA. *(moving down centre)* Where's Edward?

LADY ANGKATELL. I think he took his gun and went up to the woods. Henry was going with him – but someone came to see him about something.

HENRIETTA. I see. *(She stands lost in thought.)*

(Two revolver shots are heard off right.)

LADY ANGKATELL. Doing any work this morning?

HENRIETTA. *(sitting on the sofa)* No. It's gone stale on me.

(A revolver shot is heard off right.)

LADY ANGKATELL. I think it's so clever of you, darling – doing all these odd abstract things.

HENRIETTA. I thought you didn't like them, Lucy.

LADY ANGKATELL. No, I've always thought them rather silly, But I think it's so clever of you to know they're not.

(**GERDA** *enters hurriedly left. She looks alarmed.*)

GERDA. I heard shots – quite near the house.

LADY ANGKATELL. Nothing, darling – Henry – target practice – they've got targets in what used to be the bowling alley.

HENRIETTA. *(rising)* Come and have a try, Gerda.

GERDA. Is it difficult? *(She crosses to* **HENRIETTA**.*)*

HENRIETTA. No, of course not. You just close your eyes and press the trigger and the bullet goes somewhere.

(Two shots are heard off right. **HENRIETTA** *and* **GERDA** *exit right. A shot is heard off right.* **LADY ANGKATELL** *rises, crosses to the coffee table, puts the newspaper on it, and picks up the vase and odd leaves. Two shots are heard off right.* **LADY ANGKATELL** *crosses to the waste-paper basket, drops the leaves in it, then moves to the drinks table and puts the vase on it. Two shots are*

heard off right. JOHN *enters up centre from right. He is smoking a cigarette.)*

JOHN. Has the war started?

LADY ANGKATELL. Yes, dear – no, dear. Henry. Target practice.

JOHN. He's very keen. I remember.

LADY ANGKATELL. Why don't you join them?

JOHN. *(crossing to the fireplace)* I ought to write some letters. *(He stubs out his cigarette in the ashtray on the mantelpiece.)* I wonder if you'd mind if I wrote them in here?

LADY ANGKATELL. *(easing above the sofa)* Of course. You'll find stamps in the little drawer. If you put the letters on the hall table, Gudgeon will see that they go.

JOHN. This is the best run house in England.

LADY ANGKATELL. Bless you, darling. Now let me see – *(she looks around)* where did I lay my eggs? Ah, there, by the chair.

(She picks up the basket of eggs and moves to the door left.)

JOHN. I didn't quite understand what you meant.

*(*LADY ANGKATELL *exits left.* JOHN *crosses to the writing table, and takes a note from his pocket. He reads it, then crumples it and throws it into the waste-paper basket. He sits, sighs heavily and starts to write.* VERONICA *enters up centre from left. She carries a large, very flamboyant, red suède handbag.)*

VERONICA. *(standing at the French window up centre; imperiously)* John.

JOHN. *(turning; startled)* Veronica. *(He rises.)*

VERONICA. *(moving down centre)* I sent you a note asking you to come over at once. Didn't you get it?

JOHN. *(pleasantly, but with reserve)* Yes, I got it.

VERONICA. Well, why didn't you come? I've been waiting.

JOHN. I'm afraid it wasn't convenient for me to come over this morning.

VERONICA. *(crossing to left of* **JOHN***)* Can I have a cigarette, please?

JOHN. Yes, of course. *(He offers her a cigarette from his case.) (Before he can give her a light,* **VERONICA** *takes her own lighter from her handbag and lights the cigarette herself.)*

VERONICA. I sent for you because we've got to talk. We've got to make arrangements. For our future, I mean.

JOHN. Have we a future?

VERONICA. Of course we've got a future. We've wasted ten years. There's no need to waste any more time. *(She sits on the sofa, centre of it, and puts her handbag on the right end of the sofa.)*

JOHN. *(easing to right of the sofa)* I'm sorry, Veronica. I'm afraid you've got this worked out the wrong way. I've – enjoyed meeting you again very much, but you know we don't really belong together – we're worlds apart.

VERONICA. Nonsense, John. I love you and you love me. We've always loved each other. You were very obstinate in the past. But never mind that now.

(**JOHN** *crosses above the sofa to left of it.*)

Look, our lives needn't clash. I don't mean to go back to the States for quite a while. When I've finished the picture I'm working on now, I'm going to play a straight part on the London stage. I've got a new play – Elderton's written it for me. It'll be a terrific success.

JOHN. *(politely)* I'm sure it will.

VERONICA. *(condescendingly)* And you can go on being a doctor. You're quite well known, they tell me.

JOHN. *(moving down left centre; irritably)* I am a fairly well-known consultant on certain diseases – if it interests you – but I imagine it doesn't.

VERONICA. What I mean is we can both get on with our own jobs. It couldn't have worked out better.

JOHN. *(surveying her dispassionately)* You really are the most interesting character. Don't you realize that I'm a married man – I have children?

VERONICA. *(rising and crossing to right of* **JOHN***)* Well, I'm married myself at the moment. But these things are easily arranged. A good lawyer can fix anything. *(softly)* I always did mean to marry you, darling. I can't think why I have this terrible passion for you – *(she puts her arms around* **JOHN***'s neck)* but there it is.

JOHN. *(shaking her off; brusquely)* I'm sorry, Veronica. *(He moves to the fireplace.)* It's out of the question.

VERONICA. But I tell you a good lawyer can easily fix...

JOHN. No good lawyer is going to fix anything. Your life and mine have nothing in common.

VERONICA. *(moving to right of* **JOHN** *and facing him)* Not after last night?

JOHN. You're not a child, Veronica. You've had two husbands and, I've no doubt, a good many lovers. What does "last night" mean exactly? Nothing at all, and you know it.

VERONICA. If you'd seen your face, yesterday evening – when I came through that window – we might have been back in the South of France all those years ago.

JOHN. I was back in the South of France. *(gently)* Try to understand, Veronica. You came to me last night straight out of the past. I'd been thinking about you. Wondering whether I'd been as wise a young man as I'd thought myself – or whether I'd simply been a coward. And suddenly – there you were – like a dream come to life. But you were a dream. Today I'm back in the present, a man ten years older. *(He crosses to left of the sofa.)* A man you don't know and probably wouldn't like very much if you did know him.

VERONICA. Are you telling me that you prefer your wife to *me?*

JOHN. Yes – yes, I am. *(He sits on the sofa at the left end of it.)* I've suddenly realized how very much fonder I am of her than I knew. When I got back to this house last night – or in the early hours of the morning – I suddenly saw how stupidly I'd risked losing everything

in the world I need. Fortunately, Gerda was asleep.
She'd no idea what time I got back. She believes I left
you quite early.

VERONICA. Your wife must be a very credulous woman.

JOHN. She loves me – and she trusts me.

VERONICA. She's a fool! *(She crosses to left of the sofa.)* And
anyway I don't believe a word of what you say. You love
me.

JOHN. I'm sorry, Veronica.

VERONICA. *(breaking down centre; incredulously)* You *don't* love
me?

JOHN. I've been perfectly frank with you. You are a very
beautiful and very seductive woman, Veronica – *(he
rises and moves up right of the sofa)* but I don't love you.

VERONICA. *(furiously)* You *belong* to me, John. *(She moves
below the sofa.)* You always have. Ever since I got to
England, I've been thinking about you, planning how
best to meet you again. *(She kneels on the sofa.)* Why do
you think I took this idiotic cottage down here? Simply
because I found out that you often came down for
weekends with the Angkatells.

JOHN. So it *was* all planned last night. *(He crosses above the
sofa to right of the armchair left centre.)* I noticed your
lighter was working this morning.

VERONICA. *(rising and turning)* You belong to me.

JOHN. *(coldly angry)* I don't belong to anyone. Where do
you get this idea that you can own another human
being? I loved you once and I wanted you to marry me
and share my life. *(He moves to the fireplace and stands
with his back to it.)* You wouldn't.

VERONICA. My life and my career were much more
important than yours. Anyone can be a doctor. *(She
stubs out her cigarette in the ashtray on the coffee table.)*

JOHN. Are you really quite as important as you think?

VERONICA. *(crossing to right of* JOHN*)* If I'm not right at the
top yet, I will be.

JOHN. I wonder. I rather doubt it. There's something lacking in you, Veronica – what is it? Warmth – generosity – you give nothing. You take – take – take all the time.

VERONICA. *(speaking in a low voice convulsed with rage)* You turned me down ten years ago. You've turned me down today. My God, I'll make you suffer for it!

JOHN. I'm sorry if I've hurt you, Veronica. You're very lovely, my dear, and I once cared for you very much. Can't we leave it at that?

VERONICA. No. *(She crosses to the French windows up centre, turns and stands in the window.)* You be careful of yourself, John Cristow. I hate you more than I ever thought it possible to hate anyone.

JOHN. *(annoyed)* Oh!

VERONICA. And don't fool yourself that I believe you're turning me down because of your *wife*. It's that other woman.

JOHN. What other woman?

VERONICA. The one who came through that door last night and stood looking at you. If I can't have you, nobody else shall have you, John. Understand that.

(She exits angrily up centre to left, leaving her handbag on the sofa. JOHN stands looking after her for a moment, then crosses to the writing table, picks up the letter he has been writing, tears it up and puts it in the waste-paper basket. GUDGEON enters right, crosses to left of the sofa, turns and sees JOHN.)

GUDGEON. I beg your pardon, sir, do you know where her ladyship is?

JOHN. They're all down in the target alley, I believe.

GUDGEON. They finished shooting some time ago, sir.

(JOHN takes VERONICA's note from his pocket, screws it up, drops it in the direction of the waste-paper basket but it misses and falls alongside.)

JOHN. *(moving to the bookshelves above the drinks table)* Then they must be in the garden somewhere.

(GUDGEON crosses below the sofa, picks up the crumpled note, puts it in the waste-paper basket, then picks up the waste-paper basket, crosses and exits left. JOHN selects a book from the bookshelves, moves above the sofa and glances at the opening pages. There is a noise off from the left end of the terrace up centre. JOHN drops the book on the sofa, goes on to the terrace, faces left, and gives a sudden start of alarm.)

Why! What are you doing? Put that down. Why you...

(The sound of a revolver shot is heard up centre. JOHN staggers down the steps, tries to cross to the door left, then collapses on the floor down left centre. A revolver is tossed on to the terrace up centre from left. There is a pause, then GERDA enters quickly down left. She carries her leathercraft bag. She runs to left of JOHN.)

GERDA. John – oh, John! *(She crosses up centre, goes on to the terrace, picks up the revolver, looks off left, then stands at the top of the steps, facing front.)*

(GUDGEON enters hurriedly left. A moment later SIR HENRY enters right. He is followed on by MIDGE.)

SIR HENRY. *(crossing to right of JOHN)* What's happened?

(GUDGEON moves to left of JOHN.)

Cristow! Cristow! Good God, what's happened? *(He kneels beside JOHN.)*

MIDGE. *(moving above the sofa)* Gerda – John – what is it?

GUDGEON. *(kneeling left of JOHN)* Dr. Cristow, sir – what is it?

SIR HENRY. *(raising JOHN's head and shoulders)* He's been wounded. *(He feels JOHN's heart.)*

(JOHN is still breathing. GUDGEON rises and eases left.)

GUDGEON. Wounded? How did it happen?

SIR HENRY. Ring for a doctor, Gudgeon.

(**GUDGEON** *crosses to the writing table and lifts the telephone receiver.*)

MIDGE. Is he dead?

SIR HENRY. No.

(**LADY ANGKATELL** *enters left.* **HENRIETTA** *enters right.*)

HENRIETTA. I heard – a shot. (*She kneels down right of* JOHN.) John – John.

(**EDWARD** *enters up centre from left and stands right of the French windows.* **JOHN** *opens his eyes and looks at* **HENRIETTA.**)

JOHN. (*trying to raise himself; in a loud urgent voice*) Henrietta – Henrietta... (*He collapses.*)

(**SIR HENRY** *feels* **JOHN**'s *heart, then looks at* **HENRIETTA** *and* **GERDA.**)

GERDA. (*moving below the armchair left centre; hysterically*) He's dead – he's dead. John's dead.

(**HENRIETTA** *moves to right of* **GERDA** *and takes the revolver from her.* **LADY ANGKATELL** *moves to left of* **GERDA** *and puts her arms around her.*)

John's dead.

(*The curtain begins to fall.*)

GUDGEON. (*into the telephone*) Get me Dr Murdock.

(*curtain*)

Scene II

(Scene – the same. Later the same day.)

(When the curtain rises, the weather has changed, the wind is rising and the sky is overcast. The windows are closed with the exception of the right side of the French windows up centre. **LADY ANGKATELL** *is seated on the sofa at the right end, knitting.* **MIDGE** *is seated on the chair down right.* **EDWARD** *is seated in the armchair left centre, doing "The Times" crossword.* **HENRIETTA** *is standing on the terrace up centre. After a while* **HENRIETTA** *moves down centre. She pauses as the clock strikes two, then paces below the sofa to right and gazes out of the window right.)*

LADY ANGKATELL. I knew the weather was too good to last. I wish I knew what to do about meals. This Inspector person and the other one – does one send them something in on a tray? Or do they have a meal with us later?

*(***HENRIETTA** *turns.)*

The police aren't at all as they are in books. This Inspector Colquhoun, for instance, well he's a *gentleman.* I know one mustn't say that these days – it annoys people – but he is. *(She pauses.)*

*(***HENRIETTA** *crosses above the sofa to left.)*

(suddenly) St Albans!

*(***EDWARD** *and* **HENRIETTA** *look at* **LADY ANGKATELL** *in surprise.)*

HENRIETTA. What about St Albans? *(She moves to the alcove.)*

LADY ANGKATELL. No, no, Hendon. The police college. Quite unlike our local Inspector Jackson, who is very nice, but such a heavy accent, and such a heavy moustache.

(HENRIETTA opens the curtain of the alcove, switches on the light and stands right of the arch, looking off left at the statue.)

MIDGE. Why did they send someone down from Scotland Yard? I thought the local people always dealt with things first.

EDWARD. This is the Metropolitan area.

MIDGE. Oh, I see.

(HENRIETTA moves to the fireplace, leaving the alcove curtain open and light on.)

LADY ANGKATELL. I don't think his wife looks after him properly. I imagine she's the kind of woman that's always cleaning the house, and doesn't bother to cook.

EDWARD. Inspector Colquhoun?

LADY ANGKATELL. No, no, dear. Inspector Jackson. I shouldn't think Colquhoun was married. Not yet. He's quite attractive.

HENRIETTA. They're a long time in with Henry.

LADY ANGKATELL. The worst of murder is it does upset the servants so.

(HENRIETTA crosses above the sofa to the window right.)

We were to have duck for lunch. Still, cold duck can be quite nice. I suppose one couldn't sit down and have a little bite, could one? *(She pauses.)* No.

MIDGE. It was all horrible. *(She shivers.)* It's dreadful having to sit in here.

LADY ANGKATELL. Well, darling, we've got to sit in here. There is nowhere else to sit.

(HENRIETTA turns and crosses below the sofa to the fireplace.)

First they turn us out of here and take photographs, then they herd us back in here and make the dining-room their headquarters, and now this Inspector Colquhoun is in the study with Henry.

(There is a pause. HENRIETTA turns and faces the fireplace.)

What does one do about Gerda, do you think? Something on a tray? A little strong soup, perhaps?

MIDGE. *(rising and moving to the window right; vehemently)* Really, Lucy, you're quite inhuman. *(She gazes out of the window.)*

LADY ANGKATELL. *(surprised)* Darling, it's all very upsetting, but one has to go on with meals and things. Excitement even makes one rather hungry – rather sick, too.

MIDGE. Yes, I know. That's just what one does feel.

LADY ANGKATELL. Reading about murders in newspapers gives one no idea how trying they can be. I feel as though I'd walked about fifteen miles. Just think, we'll be in the *News of the World* next week – perhaps even tomorrow.

EDWARD. I never see the *News of the World.*

LADY ANGKATELL. Don't you? Oh, I always do. We pretend to get it for the servants, but Gudgeon is very understanding. He doesn't take it to the servants' hall before the evening. You should read it, Edward. You'd be amazed at the number of old colonels who make improper advances to nursemaids.

(GUDGEON enters left. He carries a tray of coffee and sandwiches.)

Ah! *(She moves along the sofa and sits centre of it.)*

GUDGEON. *(crossing to the coffee table)* Mrs. Medway thought you might like some sandwiches and coffee in here, m'lady – *(he puts the tray on the coffee table)* as the dining-room is still occupied.

(He moves the table in to **LADY ANGKATELL.**) Shall I take something in to the study to Sir Henry and the police officer?

LADY ANGKATELL. Yes, yes, thank you, Gudgeon. I'm a little worried about Mrs. Cristow.

GUDGEON. Simmonds has already taken her up some tea, and some thin bread and butter and a boiled egg, m'lady. *(He turns and crosses to the door left.)*

LADY ANGKATELL. Thank you, Gudgeon. I had forgotten about the eggs, Gudgeon. I meant to do something about them.

GUDGEON. *(stopping and turning)* I have already attended to that, m'lady. *(with a trace of emphasis) Quite* satisfactorily, I think. You need have no further anxiety.

(He exits left.)

LADY ANGKATELL. I don't know what I should do without him. These substantial sandwiches are just what is needed – not as heartless as a sit-down meal, and yet...

MIDGE. *(starting to cry; hysterically)* Oh, Lucy – don't!

(LADY ANGKATELL looks surprised. EDWARD rises, crosses to the drinks table, puts his paper and pencil on it, then moves to MIDGE and puts an arm around her as she sobs unrestrainedly.)

EDWARD. Midge...

LADY ANGKATELL. Poor dear. It's all been too much for her.

EDWARD. Don't worry, Midge. It's all right. Come and sit down. *(He leads her to the sofa and sits her at the right end of it.)*

MIDGE. I'm sorry to be such a fool.

EDWARD. We understand.

MIDGE. I've lost my handkerchief.

(LADY ANGKATELL pours out four cups of coffee.)

EDWARD. *(handing MIDGE his handkerchief)* Here – have mine.

MIDGE. Thank you.

EDWARD. *(moving to the coffee table)* And have some coffee.

MIDGE. No, I don't want anything.

EDWARD. Yes, you do. *(He hands MIDGE a cup of coffee.)* Come on now – drink this. It'll make you feel better.

LADY ANGKATELL. Some coffee, Henrietta?

HENRIETTA. Yes, thank you. Shouldn't one of us go up to Gerda?

(EDWARD *picks up a cup of coffee and crosses with it to*
HENRIETTA.)

LADY ANGKATELL. My dear child, one doesn't know what
to think.

(EDWARD *moves to the coffee table, picks up a cup of
coffee for himself and eases up centre.*)

One doesn't even know what her reactions *are*. How
would one feel if one had just killed one's husband?
One simply doesn't know.

HENRIETTA. Aren't we assuming rather too readily that
Gerda *has* killed her husband?

(*There is an awkward pause.* EDWARD *looks at* LADY
ANGKATELL *and shifts uneasily.* LADY ANGKATELL
looks searchingly at HENRIETTA, *trying to make up her
mind about something.*)

EDWARD. Well, we found her standing over his body with
the revolver in her hand. I imagined there was no
question about it.

HENRIETTA. We haven't heard yet what she has to say.

EDWARD. It seems self-evident to me.

(HENRIETTA *moves up centre and goes on to the terrace.*)

LADY ANGKATELL. Mind you, she had every provocation.
John behaved in a most barefaced manner. After all,
there are ways of doing these things. Being unfaithful,
I mean.

(GERDA *enters left. She is very shaky and incoherent.
She carries her leather craft bag.*)

GERDA. (*looking around apologetically*) I – I really couldn't lie
down any longer. I felt – so restless.

LADY ANGKATELL. (*rising and moving to* GERDA) No, of
course not. (*She leads her to the sofa and sits her at the left
end of it.*) Come and sit here, my dear. (*She moves above
the sofa.*) Midge, that little cushion.

(MIDGE rises, puts her cup on the writing table, then takes the cushion from the chair down right and hands it to LADY ANGKATELL.)

LADY ANGKATELL *(cont., to GERDA)* Put your feet up. *(She puts the cushion behind GERDA's head.)* We were just about to have some sandwiches. Would you like one?

GERDA. No, no, thank you. I – I am only just beginning to realize it. I haven't been able to feel – I still can't feel – that John is really *dead*. That I shall never see him again. Who could possibly have killed him?

(They all look embarrassed. SIR HENRY enters left. He is followed on by INSPECTOR COLQUHOUN, who is a thoughtful, quiet man with charm and a sense of humour. His personality is sympathetic. He must not be played as a comedy part. SIR HENRY has a filled pipe in his hand.)

SIR HENRY. *(moving to the fireplace)* Inspector Colquhoun would like to talk to Gerda, my dear. *(He turns.)* Could you take him up and... *(He sees GERDA and breaks off.)*

LADY ANGKATELL. This is Mrs. Cristow, Mr. Colquhoun.

(The INSPECTOR crosses to left of the sofa.)

GERDA. *(nervously)* Yes – yes – I – you want to talk to me? About John's death?

INSPECTOR. I don't want to distress you, Mrs. Cristow, but I would like to ask you a few questions. You're not bound to answer them unless you wish to do so, and you are entitled, if you like, to have your solicitor present before you say anything at all.

SIR HENRY. That is what I should advise, Gerda.

GERDA. *(putting her feet to the ground and sitting up)* A solicitor? But why a solicitor? A solicitor wouldn't know anything about John's death.

INSPECTOR. Any statement you choose to make...

GERDA. I want to tell you. It's all so bewildering – like a bad dream. I haven't been able to cry, even. I just don't feel anything at all.

SIR HENRY. It's the shock.

GERDA. You see, it all happened so suddenly. I'd gone back to the house. I was just coming downstairs to fetch my leathercraft bag, and I heard a shot – came in here and there was John – lying all twisted up – and blood – blood...

(MIDGE moves to the chair down right and sits.)

INSPECTOR. What time was this, Mrs. Cristow?

(LADY ANGKATELL and MIDGE exchange looks.)

GERDA. I don't know. It might have been twelve o'clock – or half past.

INSPECTOR. Where had you been before you came downstairs?

GERDA. In my room.

INSPECTOR. Had you just got up?

GERDA. No. I'd been up for about three-quarters of an hour. I'd been outside. Sir Henry was very kindly teaching me how to shoot – but I did it so badly I couldn't hit the target at all.

(LADY ANGKATELL and MIDGE exchange looks.)

Then I walked round a little – for exercise – came back to the house for my leatherwork bag, went upstairs, came down and then – as I told you – I heard a shot and came in here – and there was John dead.

HENRIETTA. *(coming down the steps up centre)* Dying. *(She moves to the drinks table, puts down her cup, takes a cigarette from the box on the table and lights it from the one she is smoking.)*

(They all look at HENRIETTA.)

GERDA. I thought he was dead. There was the blood and the revolver. I picked it up...

INSPECTOR. Why did you pick it up, Mrs. Cristow?

(There is a tense pause. All lock at the INSPECTOR.)

GERDA. I don't know.

INSPECTOR. You shouldn't have touched it, you know.

GERDA. Shouldn't I?

(**MIDGE** *takes a cigarette from the case in her bag.*)

INSPECTOR. And then what happened?

GERDA. Then the others all came in and I said, "John's dead – somebody's killed John." But who could have killed him? Who could possibly have wanted to kill him?

(**SIR HENRY** *strikes a match suddenly and lights his pipe.* **EDWARD** *looks at him for a moment.*)

John was the best of men, so good, so kind. He did everything for everyone. He sacrificed himself. Why, his patients all adored him. It must have been some sort of accident, it must – it must.

MIDGE. Couldn't it have been suicide?

(**MIDGE** *feels in her bag for her lighter.*)

INSPECTOR. No. (*He crosses below the sofa to right of it.*) The shot was fired from at least four feet away.

GERDA. But it must have been an accident.

INSPECTOR. It wasn't an accident, Mrs. Cristow. (*He takes his lighter from his pocket and lights* **MIDGE***'s cigarette.*) There was no disagreement between you?

GERDA. Between John and me? No.

(**MIDGE** *rises and crosses above the sofa to the steps up centre*)

INSPECTOR. Are you sure of that?

GERDA. He was a little annoyed with me when we drove down here. I change gear so badly. I – I don't know how it is, whenever I'm in the car with him, I never seem to do anything right. I get nervous.

INSPECTOR. There was no serious disagreement? No – quarrel?

GERDA. Quarrel? Between John and me? No, Inspector. No, John and I never quarrelled. He was so good, so kind. *(She starts to cry.)* I shall never see him again.

*(**MIDGE** moves to left of the sofa.)*

LADY ANGKATELL.		*(To* **GERDA.**) Darling. *(She turns to **MIDGE**.)* Midge, dear.
MIDGE.	*(together).*	*(Moving to **GERDA** and helping her to rise.)* I'll take her up, Lucy.
INSPECTOR.		That's all, Mrs. Cristow.
GERDA.		If I could go back to my room—please.

*(The **INSPECTOR** nods and moves up right.)*

MIDGE. Yes. Come and have a rest. You'll feel better.

LADY ANGKATELL. Tell Simmonds – a hot-water bottle.

*(**MIDGE** leads **GERDA** to the door left and they exit together.)*

*(to the **INSPECTOR**)* She adored him.

INSPECTOR. Just so. *(He moves down right.)* Now, I should like to talk to you all, one at a time. Perhaps, Lady Angkatell, you wouldn't mind…?

LADY ANGKATELL. *(delighted)* Oh no, of course not, Inspector. I want to do everything I can to help you. *(She eases to left of the sofa.)* I feel that we must all be very very co-operative.

INSPECTOR. That's certainly what we should like.

LADY ANGKATELL. *(confidentially)* Actually, this is my first murder.

INSPECTOR. Indeed?

LADY ANGKATELL. Yes, an old story to you, of course. I suppose you're always rushing about here and there, arresting people, sending out flying squads?

INSPECTOR. We're not quite so dynamic as all that.

SIR HENRY. My wife is very fond of going to the pictures, Inspector.

INSPECTOR. I'm afraid in real life it's much more boring than on the screen. *(He crosses below* LADY ANGKATELL *to left centre.)* We just go on asking people a lot of rather dull questions.

LADY ANGKATELL. *(radiantly)* And now you want to ask *me* a lot of questions. Well, I shall do everything I can to help you. As long as you don't ask me what time anything was, or where I was, or what I was doing. Because that's something I never remember – even when I was quite tiny.

SIR HENRY. Don't discourage the Inspector too much, my dear. *(He moves to the door left and opens it.)* May I come along, too?

INSPECTOR. I should be pleased, Sir Henry.

SIR HENRY. My wife's remarks are sometimes rather hard to follow. I can act as interpreter.

(LADY ANGKATELL *crosses and exits left. The* INSPECTOR *and* SIR HENRY *follow her off.* HENRIETTA *moves on to the terrace up centre and stands in the window.* EDWARD *watches her in silence for a few moments. She pays no attention to him.)*

EDWARD. It's not so warm as yesterday.

HENRIETTA. No, no – it's cold – autumn chill.

EDWARD. You'd better come in – you'll catch cold.

HENRIETTA. I think I'll go for a walk.

EDWARD. I shouldn't.

HENRIETTA. Why?

EDWARD. *(crossing to the fireplace and putting his cup and saucer on the mantelpiece)* Well, for one thing it's going to rain – and another – they might think it odd.

HENRIETTA. You think a policeman would plod after me through the woods?

EDWARD. I really don't know. One can't tell what they're thinking – the whole thing *seems* obvious.

HENRIETTA. Gerda, you mean?

EDWARD. After all, who else is there?

HENRIETTA. *(moving to right of the armchair left centre)* Who else had a motive to kill John Cristow?

EDWARD. Yes.

HENRIETTA. Did Gerda have a motive?

EDWARD. If she found out a few things – after all, last night... *(He breaks off.)*

HENRIETTA. John and Veronica Craye, you mean?

EDWARD. *(slightly embarrassed)* Well, yes. *(impatiently)* He must have been crazy.

HENRIETTA. He was. Adolescent passion unresolved and kept in cold storage and then suddenly released. *(She crosses to the coffee table and stubs out her cigarette in the ashtray.)* He was crazy all right.

EDWARD. She's a remarkably good-looking woman in a rather hard obvious sort of way. But I can't see anything to lose your head about.

HENRIETTA. I don't suppose John could – this morning.

EDWARD. *(turning to face the fire)* It's an unsavoury business.

HENRIETTA. Yes. *(She crosses to right of the sofa.)* I think I will go for a walk.

EDWARD. Then I'll come with you.

HENRIETTA. I'd rather be alone.

EDWARD. *(moving below the sofa)* I'm coming with you.

HENRIETTA. Don't you understand? I want to be alone – with my dead.

EDWARD. I'm sorry. *(He pauses.)* Henrietta, I haven't said anything – I thought you'd rather I didn't. But you do know, don't you, how sorry I am?

HENRIETTA. Sorry? *(with a bitter smile)* That John Cristow's dead?

EDWARD. *(taken aback)* I meant – sorry for you. I know it's been a great shock.

HENRIETTA. *(bitterly)* Shock? Oh, but I'm tough, Edward. I can stand shocks. Was it a shock to you? *(She crosses above the sofa to left of it.)* I wonder what you felt when you saw him lying there? Glad, I suppose. *(accusingly)* Were you glad?

EDWARD. Of course I wasn't glad. Cristow and I had nothing in common, but...

HENRIETTA. You had me in common. You were both fond of me, weren't you? But it didn't make a bond between you – quite the opposite.

EDWARD. Henrietta – don't speak so bitterly. I do feel for you in your loss – your grief.

HENRIETTA. *(sombrely)* Is it grief?

EDWARD. What do you mean?

HENRIETTA. *(to herself)* So quick. *(She crosses to the fireplace.)* It can happen so quickly. One moment living – breathing – and – the next – dead – gone – emptiness. Oh, the emptiness. And here we are eating sandwiches and drinking coffee, and calling ourselves alive. And John, who was more alive than any of us, is dead. *(She moves centre.)* I say the word, you know, over and over again to myself. Dead – dead – dead – dead – and soon it hasn't any meaning, *(She crosses to the chair down right.)* it hasn't any meaning at all. Just a funny little word like the breaking of a rotten branch. Dead – dead – dead – dead – dead.

EDWARD. *(moving in to* **HENRIETTA** *and taking her by the shoulders)* Henrietta. Henrietta, stop it – stop!

HENRIETTA. *(regaining control of herself; quietly)* Didn't you know I'd feel like this? What did you think? That I'd sit crying gently into a nice little pocket handkerchief while you held my hand? That it would all be a great shock for me, but that presently I'd begin to get over it?

*(*** EDWARD*** drops his arms.)*

And you'd comfort me very nicely? You are nice, Edward – *(She crosses below him and sits on the sofa at the left end of it.)* but it's not enough.

EDWARD. *(deeply hurt)* Yes, I've always known that.

HENRIETTA. What do you think it's been like here today? With John dead and nobody caring but me and Gerda. With you glad, and Midge upset, and Henry worried, and Lucy enjoying, in a delicate sort of way, the *News of the World* come from print into real life. Can't you see how like a fantastic nightmare it is?

EDWARD. *(moving up right)* Yes, I see.

HENRIETTA. At this moment nothing seems real to me but John. I know – I'm being a brute to you, Edward, but I can't help it, I can't help resenting that John who was so alive is dead... *(She breaks off.)*

EDWARD. And that I – *(He turns above the sofa.)* who am half dead, am alive?

HENRIETTA. *(rising quickly and turning to face **EDWARD**)* I didn't mean that, Edward.

EDWARD. I think you did, Henrietta.

(**HENRIETTA** *makes a hopeless gesture, turns and exits right, leaving the window open.* **EDWARD** *looks after her like a man in a dream.* **MIDGE** *enters left.)*

MIDGE. *(moving left centre)* Brrr! It's cold in here.

EDWARD. *(absently)* Yes.

MIDGE. Where's everybody?

EDWARD. I don't know.

MIDGE. *(moving up centre)* Is something wrong? *(She closes the French windows up centre, then crosses and closes the window right.)* Do we want the windows open? Edward – *(She touches his hand.)* you're icy cold. *(She takes his hand and leads him to the fireplace.)* Come over here and I'll light a fire. *(She takes a box of matches from the mantelpiece, kneels and lights the fire.)*

EDWARD. *(moving to the armchair left centre; deeply moved)* You're a dear child, Midge. *(He sits.)*

MIDGE. No, not a child. Do you still have fir cones at Ainswick?

EDWARD. Oh yes, there's always a basket of them beside the fire.

MIDGE. Dear Ainswick.

EDWARD. *(looking towards the French windows right)* One shouldn't have to live there alone.

MIDGE. Did Henrietta go out?

EDWARD. Yes.

MIDGE. What an odd thing to do. It's raining.

EDWARD. She was upset. Did you know that she and John Cristow...?

MIDGE. Were having an affair? *(She rises and replaces the matches on the mantelpiece.)* Yes, of course.

EDWARD. Everybody knew, I suppose.

MIDGE. *(turning)* Everybody except Gerda.

EDWARD. Damn him!

MIDGE. *(moving to* EDWARD *and kneeling down left of him)* Darling – don't. *(She holds his arm.)*

EDWARD. Even dead – he's got her.

MIDGE. Don't, Edward – please.

EDWARD. She's changed so much – since those days at Ainswick.

MIDGE. We've all changed.

EDWARD. I haven't. I've just stayed still.

MIDGE. What about me?

EDWARD. You haven't changed.

MIDGE. *(releasing his arm and looking away; bitterly)* How do you know? You never look at me.

(EDWARD *is startled. He takes her face in his left hand.*)

I'm a woman, Edward.

(GUDGEON *enters left.* MIDGE *rises.*)

GUDGEON. The Inspector would like to see you in the dining room, sir.

EDWARD. *(rising)* Oh yes, certainly.

(He exits left. GUDGEON closes the door after him. MIDGE moves above the armchair left centre to right of it. During the ensuing dialogue, GUDGEON collects the tray from the coffee table, gets the coffee cups and saucers and puts them on it.)

MIDGE. Is Mrs. Cristow still resting?

GUDGEON. As far as I know, miss, yes. Dr Murdock left her some tablets and Simmonds has instructions to administer one every two hours.

MIDGE. Would you like one of us to go up to her?

GUDGEON. I hardly think that necessary, miss. Simmonds is quite reliable.

MIDGE. I'm sure she is.

GUDGEON. *(moving to the door left)* Thank you, miss. Thank you.

(He exits left taking the tray and coffee cups with him. MIDGE closes the door behind him. HENRIETTA enters the terrace up centre from left and taps on the window. MIDGE runs up centre, lets HENRIETTA in, then closes the window behind her.)

MIDGE. How you startled me. *(She nods right.)* I expected you to come in that way.

HENRIETTA. *(crossing to the fire)* I've been walking round and round the house. I'm glad you lit a fire.

MIDGE. *(moving to left of the sofa; accusingly)* What did you do to Edward?

HENRIETTA. *(absently)* Edward?

MIDGE. Yes, when I came in just now, he was looking dreadful – so cold and grey.

HENRIETTA. *(turning)* Midge – Midge, if you care so much for Edward, why don't you do something about him?

MIDGE. Do something? What do you mean?

HENRIETTA. *(impatiently)* I don't know. Stand on a table and shout. Draw attention to yourself. Don't you know that's the only hope with a man like Edward?

MIDGE. *(sitting on the sofa at the left end of it)* I don't think Edward will ever care for anyone but you, Henrietta.

HENRIETTA. Then it's very unintelligent of him.

MIDGE. Perhaps – but there it is.

HENRIETTA. He doesn't even know what I'm like. He just goes on caring for his idea of what I once was. Today – I hate Edward.

MIDGE. You *can't* hate Edward. *Nobody* could hate Edward.

HENRIETTA. I can.

MIDGE. But why?

HENRIETTA. Because he reminds me of a lot of things I'd like to forget.

MIDGE. What things?

HENRIETTA. Ainswick.

MIDGE. Ainswick? You want to forget Ainswick?

HENRIETTA. Yes, yes. I was happy at Ainswick. *(She moves left centre.)* Don't you understand that I can't bear just now to be reminded of a time when I was happy?

(**LADY ANGKATELL** *enters left.* **MIDGE** *rises.*)

(abruptly) I shall never go back to Ainswick.

(She moves to the door left, ignores **LADY ANGKATELL** *and exits.)*

LADY ANGKATELL. What did she say?

MIDGE. *(crossing to right)* She said she would never go back to Ainswick.

LADY ANGKATELL. *(closing the door)* Oh, I think she will, darling.

MIDGE. You mean she'll – marry Edward?

LADY ANGKATELL. Yes. *(She crosses to the drinks table, picks up the box of chocolates, then moves to left of* **MIDGE**.*)* I think so. *(cheerfully)* Now that John Cristow's out of the way.

Oh yes, I think she'll marry Edward. Everything's working out quite for the best, isn't it?

MIDGE. Perhaps John Cristow wouldn't think so.

LADY ANGKATELL. No, well I wasn't thinking of him.

(The INSPECTOR enters left. He is followed on by DETECTIVE SERGEANT PENNY. The SERGEANT is in plain clothes. He carries a notebook to which he frequently refers, and in which he makes further notes.)

INSPECTOR. Is Miss Angkatell about?

MIDGE. She went upstairs to change, I think. Shall I fetch her?

LADY ANGKATELL. *(crossing to left)* No, no, I'll go. I want to see how Gerda is. *(She offers the chocolates to the INSPECTOR.)* Sweetie? Soft centres.

INSPECTOR. No, thank you.

LADY ANGKATELL. *(offering the sweets to the SERGEANT)* There's jelly baby there.

SERGEANT. No, thank you.

(LADY ANGKATELL exits left. The SERGEANT closes the door.)

INSPECTOR. *(crossing to left of the sofa)* You're Miss Harvey, aren't you?

MIDGE. Yes. Margerie Harvey.

INSPECTOR. You don't live here? *(He indicates the sofa.)* Do sit down.

MIDGE. No, I live at twenty-seven Strathmere Mansions, W2.

INSPECTOR. But you are a relation?

MIDGE. *(sitting on the sofa at the right end of it)* My mother was Lady Angkatell's first cousin.

INSPECTOR. And where were you when the shot was fired?

MIDGE. In the garden.

INSPECTOR. You were all rather scattered, weren't you? *(He crosses above the sofa to right of it.)* Lady Angkatell had just come in from the farm. Mr. Angkatell down from the woods. You from the garden, Mrs. Cristow from her bedroom, Sir Henry from the target alley. And Miss Angkatell?

MIDGE. She'd been in the garden somewhere.

INSPECTOR. *(crossing above the sofa to left of it)* You quite boxed the compass between you all. Now, Miss Harvey, I'd like you to describe what you saw when you came in here, very carefully.

MIDGE. *(pointing left centre)* John Cristow was lying there. There was blood – Mrs. Cristow was standing with the – revolver in her hand.

INSPECTOR. And you thought she had shot him?

MIDGE. Well, frankly, yes, I did.

INSPECTOR. You had no doubt about it?

MIDGE. No, not then.

INSPECTOR. *(quickly)* But you have now. Why?

MIDGE. I suppose because I realized that I simply jumped to conclusions.

INSPECTOR. Why were you so sure she had shot him?

MIDGE. Because she had the revolver in her hand, I suppose.

INSPECTOR. But you must have thought she had some reason for shooting him. *(He looks keenly at her.)*

MIDGE. *(looking troubled)* I…

INSPECTOR. Well, Miss Harvey?

MIDGE. I don't know of any reason.

INSPECTOR. In fact, as far as you know, they were a very devoted couple?

MIDGE. Oh yes, they were.

INSPECTOR. I see. *(He crosses below the sofa to right of it.)* Let's get on. What happened next?

MIDGE. I think – yes, Sir Henry went and knelt down by him. He said he wasn't dead. He told Gudgeon to telephone for the doctor.

INSPECTOR. Gudgeon? That's the butler. So he was there too.

MIDGE. Yes, he was. Gudgeon went to the telephone and just then John Cristow opened his eyes. I think he tried to struggle up. And then – then he died. It was horrible.

INSPECTOR. And that's all?

MIDGE. Yes.

INSPECTOR. *(moving up right)* He didn't say anything at all before he died?

MIDGE. I think he said "Henrietta."

INSPECTOR. *(turning)* He said "Henrietta."

MIDGE. She – *(agitatedly)* she was just opposite him when he opened his eyes. He was looking right at her. *(She looks at the INSPECTOR as if in explanation.)*

INSPECTOR. I see. That's all for now, thank you, Miss Harvey.

MIDGE. *(rising and crossing to the door left)* Well, I'd better go and find Henrietta. Lady Angkatell is so very vague, you know. She usually forgets what she went to do.

(The SERGEANT opens the door. MIDGE exits left and the SERGEANT closes the door behind her.)

INSPECTOR. *(thoughtfully)* Lady Angkatell is so very vague.

SERGEANT. *(crossing to centre)* She's bats, if you ask me.

(The INSPECTOR holds out his hand and the SERGEANT gives him his notebook.)

INSPECTOR. I wonder. I wonder. *(He flicks over the pages of the notebook.)* Interesting discrepancies. Lady Angkatell says, *(he reads)* "He murmured something before he died, but she couldn't catch what it was."

SERGEANT. Perhaps she's deaf.

INSPECTOR. Oh no, I don't think she is. According to Sir Henry, John Cristow said "Henrietta" in a loud voice. When I put it to her – but not before – Miss Harvey says the same thing, Edward Angkatell says Cristow died without saying a word. Gudgeon does not precisely recollect. *(He moves below the sofa.)* They all know something, Penny, but they're not telling us. *(He sits on the sofa at the right end of it.)*

SERGEANT. We'll get round to it. *(He crosses to the* **INSPECTOR.** *)* Think the wife did shoot him? *(He takes his notebook from the* **INSPECTOR,** *then eases to right of the sofa.)*

INSPECTOR. Wives so often have excellent reasons for shooting their husbands that one tends to suspect them automatically.

SERGEANT. It's clear enough that all the others think she did it.

INSPECTOR. Or do they probably all *want* to think she did it?

SERGEANT. Meaning exactly?

INSPECTOR. There's an atmosphere of family solidarity in this house. They're all blood relations. Mrs. Cristow's the only outsider. Yes, I think they'd be glad to be sure she did it.

SERGEANT. *(crossing above the sofa to centre)* But you're not so sure?

INSPECTOR. Actually anyone could have shot him. There are no alibis in this case. *(He rises and stands right of the sofa.)* No times or places to check. Just look at the entrances and exits. You could shoot him from the terrace, pop round the house and – *(He indicates the window right.)* in by this window. Or through the front door and hall and in by that door, and if you say you've come from the farm or the kitchen garden or from shooting in the woods, nobody can check that statement. *(He looks through the window right.)* There are shrubs and undergrowth right up to the house. You could play hide-and-seek there for hours. *(He moves above the sofa.)* The revolver was one of those used for target practice. Anyone could have picked it up and they'd all handled it, though the only clear prints on it are those of Mrs. Cristow and Henrietta Angkatell. *(He moves left of the sofa.)* It all boils down really to what sort

of a man John Cristow was. *(He moves below the sofa.)* If
you know all about a man, you can guess who would
have wanted to murder him.

SERGEANT. We'll pick up all that in London, in Harley
Street. Secretary, servants.

INSPECTOR. *(sitting on the sofa at the left end of it)* Any luck
with the servants here?

SERGEANT. Not yet. They're the starchy kind. There's no
kitchen maid unfortunately. I always had a success with
kitchen maids. *(He moves above the armchair left centre to
the fireplace.)* There's a daily girl as under-housemaid
I've got hopes of. I'd like to put in a little more work
on her now, sir, if you don't want me.

*(The INSPECTOR nods. The SERGEANT grins and exits
left. The INSPECTOR rises, moves to the window right,
looks out for a moment, then turns, moves up centre
and goes out on to the terrace. After a few moments
he moves to the sofa and sits on it at the left end. He
becomes aware of something under the cushion behind
him, moves the cushion and picks up VERONICA's red
handbag. He opens the bag, looks into it and shows
considerable surprise. He closes the bag, rises, moves to
left of the sofa and weighs the bag in his hand. As he
does so voices are heard off left. He immediately replaces
the bag on the sofa and covers it with the cushion.)*

MIDGE. *(off left)* Oh, there you are, Henrietta. The Inspector
would like to see you.

HENRIETTA. *(off left)* Thank you, Midge. Lucy's just told me.
I'm going in to see him now.

MIDGE. *(off left)* Oh good. I thought she might forget.

*(The INSPECTOR crosses to right of the sofa. HENRIETTA
enters left.)*

HENRIETTA. *(closing the door)* You wanted to see me? *(She
crosses to the sofa and sits on it at the left end.)*

INSPECTOR. Yes, Miss Angkatell. You're a relation as well,
aren't you?

HENRIETTA. Yes, we're all cousins. It's rather confusing because Lady Angkatell married her second cousin and is actually an Angkatell herself.

INSPECTOR. Just a family party – with the exception of Dr and Mrs. Cristow?

HENRIETTA. Yes.

INSPECTOR. *(moving up right)* Will you give me your account of what happened?

HENRIETTA. I was in the flower garden. *(She points right.)* It's through there. Not very far from the house. I heard the shot and realized it came from the house and not from the target alley down below. I thought that was strange, so I came in.

INSPECTOR. By which window?

HENRIETTA. *(pointing right)* That one.

INSPECTOR. Will you describe what you saw?

HENRIETTA. Sir Henry and Gudgeon, the butler, were bending over John Cristow. Mrs. Cristow was beside them. She had the revolver in her hand.

INSPECTOR. *(moving to right of the sofa)* And you concluded that she had shot him?

HENRIETTA. Why should I think so?

INSPECTOR. Didn't you, in fact, think so?

HENRIETTA. No, I didn't.

INSPECTOR. What did you think, then?

HENRIETTA. I don't think I thought at all. It was all rather unexpected. Sir Henry told Gudgeon to call the doctor and he went over to the phone.

INSPECTOR. Who else was in the room?

HENRIETTA. Everybody, I think. No – Edward came in after I did.

INSPECTOR. Which way?

HENRIETTA. By the terrace.

INSPECTOR. And then?

HENRIETTA. And then – John died.

INSPECTOR. Was he conscious before he died?

HENRIETTA. Oh yes, he opened his eyes.

INSPECTOR. Did he say anything?

HENRIETTA. *(after a pause)* He said "Henrietta."

INSPECTOR. You knew him well?

HENRIETTA. Very well indeed.

INSPECTOR. He didn't say anything else?

HENRIETTA. No.

INSPECTOR. *(crossing above the sofa to left of it)* What happened next?

HENRIETTA. Let me see – oh yes, Gerda cried out. She was swaying, and waving the revolver about. I thought it might go off. I went and took it from her and tried to get her on to the sofa.

INSPECTOR. *(crossing to the fireplace)* Were you particularly a friend of Dr. Cristow or of Mrs. Cristow?

HENRIETTA. That's rather a difficult question to answer.

INSPECTOR. *(sympathetically and gently)* Is it, Miss Angkatell?

HENRIETTA. *(resolutely)* Well, I'll take a short cut. I was John Cristow's mistress. That's what you wanted to know, isn't it?

INSPECTOR. *(crossing to* **HENRIETTA***)* Thank you, Miss Angkatell. *(He takes a cigarette case from his pocket and offers a cigarette to* **HENRIETTA***. Gently)* I'm afraid we have to know all the facts.

HENRIETTA. *(taking a cigarette; in a dry voice)* If this particular fact has no bearing on the case, and I don't see how it can have, is there any necessity to make it public? Not only for my sake. It would give Mrs. Cristow a good deal of unnecessary pain.

INSPECTOR. *(lighting* **HENRIETTA**'s *cigarette)* Mrs. Cristow had no idea of the relationship between you and her husband?

HENRIETTA. None.

INSPECTOR. Are you sure of that?

HENRIETTA. Absolutely.

INSPECTOR. *(crossing above the sofa to right of it)* How long had you and Dr. Cristow been lovers?

HENRIETTA. I became his mistress six months ago. I did not say we were lovers.

INSPECTOR. *(looking at her with quickened interest)* I'm not sure that I know what you mean, Miss Angkatell.

HENRIETTA. I think you will know if you think about it.

INSPECTOR. There was no question of a divorce?

HENRIETTA. Certainly not. That's what I've been trying to explain. John Cristow had had affairs with other women. I was only one of – a procession. I don't think he really cared for any woman except his wife. But she wasn't the kind of woman he could talk to about his work. He was doing research work on an obscure disease.

*(The **INSPECTOR** sits on the sofa at the right end of it.)*

He was a very brilliant man, and his research work was the real passion of his life. He got into the habit of coming into my studio and talking to me about it. Actually it was a good deal above my head, but I got some books on the subject and read it up, so that I could understand better. And my questions, even if they weren't very technical, helped him to formulate his own ideas. *(She speaks naturally, as to a friend.)* And then – suddenly – I got between John and what he was thinking about. I began to affect him as a woman. He didn't want to fall in love with me – he'd been in love when he was a young man, and it had left him afraid of going through it again. No, he just wanted an affair, like other affairs he had. I think he thought that if he had an affair with me, he'd get me out of his system and not be distracted from his work any more.

INSPECTOR. And was that satisfactory to you?

HENRIETTA. No, no, of course not. But it had to do. I loved John Cristow, and I was content that he should have what he wanted.

INSPECTOR. I see. It was like that.

HENRIETTA. I've been forgetting that you're a policeman.

INSPECTOR. Policemen are quite like other men. We hear a good deal that isn't strictly relevant – perhaps it's because we're impersonal – like priests.

HENRIETTA. Yes, yes, I suppose you must learn a good deal about the human heart. *(She rises and flicks her cigarette ash into the ashtray on the coffee table. The following sentence does not ring quite true.)* So now you understand why John said "Henrietta" just before he died.

(The SERGEANT enters left.)

INSPECTOR. It's a small point, Miss Angkatell – *(he rises and stands right of the sofa)* but why did you take the revolver away from Mrs. Cristow?

HENRIETTA. I told you. I thought she was going to faint.

INSPECTOR. It was one of the revolvers used earlier for target practice. The only clear prints on it are Mrs. Cristow's and naturally – yours. *(He pauses.)* It would have been better if nobody had touched it.

HENRIETTA. One doesn't realize these things at the time. Is that all, Inspector?

INSPECTOR. Yes, thank you, Miss Angkatell, that's all for the present.

(The SERGEANT opens the door. HENRIETTA crosses and exits left. The SERGEANT closes the door behind her.)

SERGEANT. Get anything useful out of her?

INSPECTOR. She was Cristow's mistress. She told me that accounts for his saying "Henrietta" before he died.

SERGEANT. *(crossing to left of the sofa)* That seems fair enough.

INSPECTOR. If it's true.

SERGEANT. What other reason could he have for saying her name?

INSPECTOR. It could have been – an accusation.

SERGEANT. You mean she might have done him in?

INSPECTOR. *(crossing to the fireplace)* It's possible.

SERGEANT. My money's on the wife. If Mrs. Cristow had found out about her husband and this Henrietta, it gives us what we want – a motive.

INSPECTOR. Henrietta Angkatell says she didn't know.

SERGEANT. You can't be sure of that. Somebody tipped Mrs. Cristow off as like as not.

INSPECTOR. *(moving to the alcove and looking off at the statue)* She couldn't have hidden her feelings for long. She's not that kind of woman.

SERGEANT. What about the others? They're in the clear, I suppose?

INSPECTOR. There doesn't seem any reason why any of them should have wanted John Cristow dead. *(He turns and crosses above the sofa to the writing table.)* But there's a good deal we don't know yet. They're all watchful and cagey about what they say.

SERGEANT. I can't see how Sir Henry or Lady Angkatell could have any reason for wanting Cristow out of the way.

INSPECTOR. Nor the little girl – Miss Harvey. But remember that statement of Edward Angkatell's: "Did John Cristow say anything before he died? Nothing at all." A flat denial, that, of what we know to be true. Both Sir Henry and Miss Harvey say that John Cristow said "Henrietta" in quite a loud voice.

SERGEANT. You think Edward Angkatell's sweet on this Henrietta woman?

INSPECTOR. That is my idea.

SERGEANT. And was doing his best not to get her mixed up in it.

INSPECTOR. Exactly.

SERGEANT. Yes – it certainly looks like it.

INSPECTOR. *(easing below the sofa)* And granting that, Penny, it gives us another suspect.

SERGEANT. Edward Angkatell?

INSPECTOR. *(sitting on the sofa at the right end of it)* Yes. He's the nervous sort. If he cared very much for Henrietta and discovered that she was John Cristow's mistress, he's just the quiet type that goes off half-cock when everybody least expects it.

SERGEANT. Hoped he'd get her when the other man was out of the way?

INSPECTOR. We've both known cases like that.

SERGEANT. *(moving up centre)* So in your opinion it's between the three of them, Henrietta Angkatell, Edward Angkatell and the wife?

INSPECTOR. Oh, I've got a very open mind about it, Penny – a very open mind. *(He takes* **VERONICA**'s *handbag from under the cushion and holds it up.)* Just tell me what you make of this?

SERGEANT. *(moving to left of the sofa)* Lady's handbag.

INSPECTOR. Undoubtedly.

SERGEANT. We went over it when we did this room. *(He consults his notebook.)* Two pounds ten shillings in notes, seven shillings in cash, the usual lipstick, powder compact and rouge. Silver cigarette lighter. Lace handkerchief unmarked. All very Ritzy. Belongs to one of the ladies, I suppose, I couldn't say which.

(The **INSPECTOR** *rises with the bag in his hand, crosses to the fireplace and presses the bell-push.)*

I didn't go into the matter as I didn't think it important.

INSPECTOR. You think it belongs to one of the ladies in this house?

SERGEANT. *(moving up left centre)* I assumed so. Have you any reason for thinking otherwise?

INSPECTOR. Only aesthetic sense. *(He crosses to left of the sofa.)* Not in good enough taste for Lady Angkatell. Too expensive for little Miss Harvey. Far too fashionable for Mrs. Cristow. Too flamboyant for Henrietta Angkatell. It doesn't seem to me to belong to this household at all. *(He looks at the bag.)* I find it – very intriguing.

SERGEANT. *(easing to the fireplace)* I daresay I can find out who it does belong to. But as I say, the contents being nothing out of the ordinary…

INSPECTOR. Are you quite sure you've mentioned all its contents?

SERGEANT. I think so, sir.

(GUDGEON *enters left.*)

GUDGEON. You rang, sir?

INSPECTOR. Yes. Can you tell me to whom this bag belongs?

GUDGEON. *(crossing to left of the* INSPECTOR*)* I'm afraid not, sir. I don't recollect ever having seen it before. I could ask her ladyship's own maid, sir. She would probably know better than I should.

INSPECTOR. Thank you.

(GUDGEON *turns, moves to the door down left, then hesitates and turns.*)

GUDGEON. It's just occurred to me, sir, if I might make a suggestion?

INSPECTOR. By all means.

GUDGEON. *(moving left centre)* It might possibly be the property of Miss Veronica Craye.

SERGEANT. *(moving to left of* GUDGEON*)* Veronica Craye? The film star? Is she in this part of the world?

GUDGEON. *(giving the* SERGEANT *a dirty look; to the* INSPECTOR*)* She occupies the cottage a hundred yards up the lane. Dovecotes, it's called.

INSPECTOR. Has Miss Craye been here?

GUDGEON. She was here yesterday evening, sir.

INSPECTOR. And she was carrying this bag?

GUDGEON. No, sir. She was in evening dress and was carrying a white diamante bag. But I think it possible Miss Craye was here earlier this morning for a short time.

INSPECTOR. When?

GUDGEON. About midday, sir.

INSPECTOR. You saw her?

GUDGEON. I didn't see her myself, sir.

SERGEANT. Well, who did?

GUDGEON. *(with an angry glance at the* SERGEANT*)* The underhousemaid observed her from one of the bedroom windows, sir. The girl is an ardent movie fan. She was quite thrilled.

SERGEANT. I'll have a word with that girl.

(He exits left.)

INSPECTOR. Lady Angkatell didn't mention that Miss Craye had been here this morning.

GUDGEON. I don't think her ladyship was aware of Miss Craye's visit.

INSPECTOR. Who did she come to see, then?

GUDGEON. As to that, sir, I couldn't say.

(The INSPECTOR *crosses above the sofa to right of it.)*

H'm! *(He coughs.)*

INSPECTOR. *(turning to* GUDGEON*)* Yes?

GUDGEON. A note was brought over from Dovecotes for Dr. Cristow earlier in the morning. Dr. Cristow said there was no answer.

INSPECTOR. I see. What happened to that note?

GUDGEON. I think I could produce it for you, sir. I picked up some crumpled paper by the waste-paper basket.

INSPECTOR. Thank you, Gudgeon – I should be extremely obliged if you will bring it to me at once.

GUDGEON. *(turning and crossing to the door left)* Very good, sir.

INSPECTOR. I gather Dr. Cristow knew Miss Craye?

GUDGEON. It would seem so, sir. He went over to see her last night – after dinner. *(He waits expectantly.)*

INSPECTOR. When did he return?

GUDGEON. As to that, sir, I could not say. Acting on Sir Henry's instructions I left the side door unfastened when I retired to bed at twelve-fifteen A.M.

(*The* INSPECTOR *puts the bag on the writing table.*)

Up to that time Dr. Cristow had not returned.

(VERONICA *enters up centre from left.*)

VERONICA. I've just heard the news. It's awful – just awful. (*She moves above the sofa.*) Are you…?

INSPECTOR. I'm Inspector Colquhoun of Scotland Yard.

VERONICA. Then John *was* murdered?

(GUDGEON *exits abruptly left.*)

INSPECTOR. Oh yes, Miss Craye, he was murdered.

VERONICA. So you know who I am? (*She moves below the left end of the sofa.*)

INSPECTOR. I'm very fond of a good film.

VERONICA. How charming of you. (*She sits on the sofa at the left end of it.*) I'm over in England to make a picture.

INSPECTOR. (*crossing below the sofa to left centre*) Dr. Cristow was a friend of yours?

VERONICA. I hadn't seen him for years. I came over last night to borrow some matches – and the first person I saw when I came into the room was John Cristow.

INSPECTOR. Were you pleased to see him?

VERONICA. I was very pleased. It's always nice to meet an old friend.

INSPECTOR. He called on you yesterday evening, I believe?

VERONICA. Yes, I asked him to come over after dinner if he could manage it. We had a delightful talk about old times and old friends.

INSPECTOR. (*crossing to the fireplace*) What time did he leave?

VERONICA. I've really no idea. We talked for quite a while.

INSPECTOR. About old times?

VERONICA. Yes, of course a lot had happened to us both.

(The INSPECTOR *moves up centre and closes the window.)*

He'd done very well in his profession, I understand. And he'd married since I knew him.

INSPECTOR. *(easing up right)* You didn't know his wife?

VERONICA. No, no, he introduced us here last night. I gathered from what he – well, didn't exactly say, but hinted at – that his married life wasn't awfully happy.

INSPECTOR. Oh, really.

VERONICA. I think his wife was one of those dim ineffectual women who are inclined to be jealous.

INSPECTOR. *(moving to right of the sofa)* Had she any cause for jealousy?

VERONICA. Oh, don't ask me. I just thought there might have been a little trouble lately. Jealousy does make people do such dreadful things.

INSPECTOR. You think he was shot by his wife?

VERONICA. Oh, I don't really know anything about it. It was my maid – she told me that his wife had actually been found standing over him with the revolver still in her hand. But of course the wildest stories do get around in the country.

INSPECTOR. *(easing above the writing table)* This one happens to be quite true.

VERONICA. Oh, I suppose his wife found out about him and the sculptress woman.

(The SERGEANT *enters left. He carries the crumpled note.)*

INSPECTOR. Excuse me.

(The SERGEANT *crosses below the coffee table to the* INSPECTOR *and hands him the crumpled note.)*

VERONICA. Of course.

SERGEANT. *(aside to the* INSPECTOR*)* He got back at three o'clock. *(He moves up right.)*

VERONICA. I really just came over to – to…

INSPECTOR. *(picking up the handbag)* To get your bag perhaps? It *is* your bag?

VERONICA. *(disconcerted)* Oh yes. *(She rises.)* Thank you.

INSPECTOR. Just a moment.

(VERONICA resumes her seat on the sofa.)

(He refers to the note, then crosses below the sofa to left centre.) Dr. Cristow returned to this house at three A.M. this morning. Isn't that rather an unconventional hour?

VERONICA. We were talking about old times.

INSPECTOR. So you said.

VERONICA. It must have been much later than I thought.

INSPECTOR. Was that the last time you saw Dr. Cristow?

VERONICA. *(quickly)* Yes.

INSPECTOR. Are you quite sure, Miss Craye?

VERONICA. Of course I'm sure.

INSPECTOR. What about this bag of yours?

VERONICA. Oh, I must have left that last night, when I came to get the matches.

INSPECTOR. Rather large and heavy for an evening bag. *(He pauses.)* I think you left it here this morning.

VERONICA. And what makes you think that?

INSPECTOR. *(moving to the fireplace and putting the bag on the mantelpiece)* Partly this note of yours. *(He smooths out the note and reads it.)* "Please come over this morning. I must see you, Veronica." A little curt, Miss Craye. Dr. Cristow, I believe, said there was no answer. He didn't come to you – so you came here to see him, didn't you?

VERONICA. *(rising and moving to the armchair left centre; with a change of manner)* How wonderful you are! You seem to know *everything*.

INSPECTOR. Not quite everything. What happened when you came here? Did you quarrel?

VERONICA. We-ell – you couldn't call it a *quarrel* exactly. *(She sighs and sits in the armchair left centre)* Poor John.

INSPECTOR. Why poor John?

VERONICA. I didn't want to tell you. It didn't seem *fair.*

INSPECTOR. Yes?

VERONICA. John went mad – quite mad. He'd been in love
  with me years ago. He – he wanted to leave his wife
  and children – he wanted me to get a divorce and
  marry him. It's really quite frightening to think one
  can have such an effect on a man.

INSPECTOR. It must be. Very sudden and unexpected.

VERONICA. I know. Almost unbelievable. But it's possible,
  you know, never to forget – to wait and hope and plan.
  There are men like that.

INSPECTOR. *(watching her closely and moving above the armchair
  to right of it)* And women.

VERONICA. Yes – yes – I suppose so. Well, that's how he was.
  I pretended at first not to take him seriously. I told
  him he was mad. He'd said something of the kind last
  night. That's why I sent him that note. I couldn't leave
  things like that. I came over to make him realize that
  what he suggested was impossible. But he wouldn't
  listen to what I had to say. And now – he's dead. I feel
  dreadful.

  (The **SERGEANT** *clears his throat.)*

INSPECTOR. Yes, Sergeant?

SERGEANT. *(easing above the sofa; to* **VERONICA***)* I understand
  from information received that as you left by that
  window you were heard to say – *(he refers to his notebook)*
  "I hate you more than I ever thought it possible to
  hate anyone."

VERONICA. I'm sure I *never* said that. What have you been
  listening to? Servants' talk?

SERGEANT. One of your fans, Miss Crave, was hanging
  around hoping to *get* your autograph. *(Significantly.)*
  She heard a great deal of what went on in this room.

VERONICA. *(rising; angrily)* All a pack of lies. *(To the*
  INSPECTOR.*)* Can I have my bag, please?

INSPECTOR. *(crossing to the fireplace)* Certainly, Miss Craye. *(He picks up the bag.)* But I'm afraid I shall have to keep the gun.

VERONICA. Gun?

(The INSPECTOR takes a handkerchief from his pocket, puts it round his hand, opens the bag and takes out a revolver.)

INSPECTOR. Didn't you know there was a gun in your bag?

SERGEANT. *(with a step towards the INSPECTOR)* But...

(The INSPECTOR quells the SERGEANT with a glance.)

VERONICA. There wasn't a gun. It's not mine. I don't know anything about a gun.

INSPECTOR. *(examining the revolver)* Thirty-eight Smith and Wesson – the same calibre as the bullet that killed John Cristow.

VERONICA. *(angrily)* Don't you think you can frame me! *(She moves to the INSPECTOR.)* I'll see my attorney. I'll... How dare you!

INSPECTOR. *(holding out the bag)* Here's your bag, Miss Craye.

(VERONICA snatches the bag from him. She looks both angry and frightened.)

VERONICA. I won't say another word.

INSPECTOR. Very wise.

(VERONICA turns, glares at the SERGEANT, then exits hurriedly up centre to left. The INSPECTOR looks after her, twisting the revolver which he holds carefully in the handkerchief.)

SERGEANT. *(easing to right of the armchair left centre)* But, sir, I...

INSPECTOR. But me no buts, Penny. Things are not what they seem, and all the rest of it. *(He moves to the armchair left centre and sits slowly in it.)*

(The SERGEANT opens his mouth to protest.)

(He silences the **SERGEANT** *with a gesture.)* I know – I
know. Now I wonder…?

(curtain)

ACT THREE

(Scene – the same. The following Monday morning.)

(When the curtain rises, it is a fine morning, the French windows are open and a small fire burns in the grate. **GUDGEON** *ushers in the* **INSPECTOR** *and the* **SERGEANT** *left)*

GUDGEON. I will inform Sir Henry you are here, sir.

(He exits left.)

SERGEANT. *(glancing at the drinks table)* Nice flowers. *(He moves to the fireplace.)*

INSPECTOR. *(moving up centre and standing in the French windows)* Yes.

SERGEANT. *(turning and looking at the picture over the mantelpiece)* I rather like this picture. Nice house, I wonder whose it is?

INSPECTOR. That's Lady Angkatell's old home.

SERGEANT. Is it now? All sold up like everything else nowadays?

INSPECTOR. No, it belongs to Edward Angkatell. Entailed, you see.

SERGEANT. *(turning)* Why not to Sir Henry? He's got the title.

INSPECTOR. No. He's a K.C.B. He was only a second cousin.

SERGEANT. You seem to know all about the family.

INSPECTOR. *(moving down right)* I've taken the trouble to find out all I could. I thought it might have a bearing on the case.

SERGEANT. I don't quite see how. *(He eases left centre.)* Anyway, we're getting places at last – or aren't we?

INSPECTOR. Aren't we is probably right.

(**DORIS** *enters up centre from left.*)

DORIS. *(standing in the French windows)* Ssh!

SERGEANT. Hullo.

DORIS. *(moving centre; conspiratorially)* I come round this way because I didn't want Mr. Gudgeon to spot me. They say out there it's common to have anything to do with the police, but what I say is let justice be done.

SERGEANT. That's the spirit, my girl. And who says it's common to have anything to do with the police?

DORIS. *(turning to the* **SERGEANT***)* Mrs. Medway – the cook. She said it was bad enough anyway to have police in the house and a thing that had never happened to her before and she was afraid she wasn't going to have a light hand with her pastry. *(She pauses for breath.)* And if it wasn't for her ladyship she'd give in her notice, but she couldn't leave her ladyship in the lurch. *(She crosses to left of the sofa. To the* **INSPECTOR***)* All potty about her ladyship they are.

SERGEANT. Well, come to the part about justice being done.

DORIS. *(turning and crossing to right of the* **SERGEANT***)* It's what I seen with my own eyes.

SERGEANT. And very nice eyes they are, too.

DORIS. *(nudging the* **SERGEANT***)* Oh, go on! Well, Saturday afternoon it was – the very day of the murder. I went to shut the bedroom windows because it looked like rain, and I happened to glance over the banisters, and what did I see?

SERGEANT. Well – what did you see?

DORIS. I saw Mr. Gudgeon standing in the front hall with a revolver in his hand and he looked ever so peculiar. Gave me quite a turn it did.

INSPECTOR. Gudgeon?

DORIS. *(moving to left of the sofa)* Yes, sir. And it come to me as perhaps *he* was the murderer.

INSPECTOR. Gudgeon!

DORIS. *(crossing below the sofa to left of the* INSPECTOR*)* And I
hope I've done right in coming to you, but what they'll
say to me in the servants' hall I don't know, but what I
felt was – let—

SERGEANT.			*(Moving below the sofa.)* Justice be done.
	(together).		
DORIS.			–justice be done.

SERGEANT. You did quite right, my girl.

DORIS. And what I feel is... *(She breaks off and listens.)*
Someone's coming. *(She moves quickly up centre.)* I must
hop it. I'm supposed to be counting the laundry.

(She exits up centre to left.)

SERGEANT. *(moving up centre and looking after* DORIS*)* That's
a useful girl. She's the one who was hanging about for
Miss Craye's autograph.

(SIR HENRY enters left.)

INSPECTOR. Good morning, Sir Henry.

SIR HENRY. *(crossing to left of the sofa)* Good morning,
Inspector.

SERGEANT. Good morning, sir.

(SIR HENRY nods to the SERGEANT.)

SIR HENRY. *(to the INSPECTOR)* You wanted to see me?

INSPECTOR. *(crossing to left centre)* Yes, Sir Henry. We wanted
some further information.

SIR HENRY. Yes?

INSPECTOR. Sir Henry, you have a considerable collection
of firearms, mostly pistols and revolvers. I wanted to
know *if* any of them are missing.

SIR HENRY. *(sitting on the sofa at the left end of it)* I don't
quite understand. I have already told you that I took
two revolvers and one pistol down to the target alley
on Saturday morning, and that I subsequently found
that one of them, a thirty-eight Smith and Wesson, was

missing. I identified this missing revolver as the one that Mrs. Cristow was holding just after the murder.

INSPECTOR. That is quite correct, Sir Henry. According to Mrs. Cristow's statement, she picked it up from the floor by her husband's body. We assumed, perhaps naturally, that *that* was the gun with which Dr. Cristow was shot.

SIR HENRY. Do you mean – it *wasn't?*

INSPECTOR. We have now received the report of our ballistics expert. Sir Henry, the bullet that killed Dr. Cristow was *not* fired from that gun.

SIR HENRY. You astound me.

INSPECTOR. Yes, it's extremely odd. The bullet was of the right calibre, but that was definitely not the gun used.

SIR HENRY. But may I ask, Inspector, why you should assume that the murder weapon came from my collection?

INSPECTOR. I don't assume it, Sir Henry – but I must check up before looking elsewhere.

SIR HENRY. *(rising and crossing to left)* Yes, I see that. Well, I can tell you what you want to know in a very few moments.

(He exits left.)

SERGEANT. He doesn't know anything.

INSPECTOR. *(moving up centre)* So it seems. *(He goes on to the terrace and stands looking off left)*

SERGEANT. What time's the inquest?

INSPECTOR. Twelve o'clock. There's plenty of time.

SERGEANT. Just routine evidence and an adjournment. It's all fixed up with the coroner, I suppose?

*(**MIDGE** enters left. She wears her hat and coat, and carries her handbag, gloves and suitcase.)*

INSPECTOR. *(turning)* Are you leaving, Miss Harvey?

MIDGE. *(crossing to centre)* I have to get up to town immediately after the inquest.

INSPECTOR. *(moving to right of* **MIDGE***)* I'm afraid I must ask you not to leave here today.

MIDGE. But that's very awkward. You see, I work in a dress shop. And if I'm not back by two-thirty there'll be an awful to-do.

INSPECTOR. I'm sorry, Miss Harvey. You can say you are acting on police instructions.

MIDGE. That won't go down very well, I can tell you. *(She crosses below the sofa to the writing table, puts her handbag and gloves on it and stands the case on the floor above the writing table.)* Oh well, I suppose I'd better ring up now and get it over. *(She lifts the telephone receiver. Into the telephone.)* Hello…

(The voice of the **OPERATOR** *is reasonably audible.)*

OPERATOR. Number please.

MIDGE. Regent four-six-nine-two, please.

OPERATOR. What is your number?

MIDGE. Dowfield two-two-one.

(The **INSPECTOR** *eases to left of the sofa and looks at the* **SERGEANT***.)*

OPERATOR. Dowfield two-two-one. There's a twenty-minute delay on the line.

MIDGE. Oh!

OPERATOR. Shall I keep the call in?

MIDGE. Yes, keep the call in, please. You'll ring me?

OPERATOR. Yes.

MIDGE. Thank you. *(She replaces the receiver.)*

*(***SIR HENRY** *enters left.)*

SIR HENRY. Do you mind leaving us, Midge?

MIDGE. Of course – but I'm expecting a call. *(She picks up her suitcase and crosses to left.)*

SIR HENRY. I'll give you a hail when it comes through, unless they forget all about it.

*(***MIDGE** *exits left.* **SIR HENRY** *closes the door behind her.)*

(He crosses to left of the INSPECTOR.*)* A second thirty-eight Smith and Wesson exhibit in a brown leather holster is missing from my study.

INSPECTOR. *(taking a revolver from his pocket)* Would it be this gun, Sir Henry?

(SIR HENRY, *surprised, takes the revolver from the* INSPECTOR *and carefully examines it.)*

SIR HENRY. Yes – yes, this is it. Where did you find it?

INSPECTOR. That doesn't matter for the moment. But the shot that killed Dr. Cristow was fired from that gun. May I speak to your butler, Sir Henry? *(He holds out his hand for the revolver.)*

SIR HENRY. *(handing the revolver to the* INSPECTOR*)* Of course. *(He turns, crosses to the fireplace and presses the bell-push.)* Do you want to speak to him in here?

INSPECTOR. *(putting the revolver in his pocket)* If you please, Sir Henry.

SIR HENRY. Do you want me to go away or to remain? I should prefer to remain. Gudgeon is a very old and valued servant.

INSPECTOR. I would prefer you to be here, Sir Henry.

(GUDGEON *enters left.)*

GUDGEON. You rang, Sir Henry?

SIR HENRY. Yes, Gudgeon. *(He indicates the* INSPECTOR.*)*

(GUDGEON *looks politely at the* INSPECTOR.*)*

INSPECTOR. Gudgeon, have you lately had a pistol or a revolver in your possession?

(SIR HENRY *sits in the armchair left centre.)*

GUDGEON. *(crossing to left of the* INSPECTOR; *imperturbably)* I don't think so, sir. I don't own any firearms.

SERGEANT. *(reading from his notebook)* "I happened to glance over the banisters and I saw Mr. Gudgeon standing in the front hall with a revolver –

(GUDGEON *reacts by clenching his fists.)*

– in his hand and he looked ever so peculiar…"

(The INSPECTOR *looks at the* SERGEANT, *who breaks off abruptly.)*

GUDGEON. That is quite correct, sir. I'm sorry it slipped my memory.

INSPECTOR. Perhaps you will tell us exactly what occurred.

GUDGEON. Certainly, sir. It was about one o'clock on Saturday. Normally of course I should have been bringing in luncheon, but owing to a murder having taken place a short time before, household routine was disorganized. As I was passing through the front hall, I noticed one of Sir Henry's pistols, a small Derringer it was, sir, lying on the oak chest there. I didn't think it should be left lying about, so I picked it up and subsequently took it to the master's study and put it back in its proper place. I may add, sir, that I have no recollection of having looked peculiar.

INSPECTOR. *(moving to right of the sofa)* You say you put the gun in Sir Henry's study? *(He moves below the sofa and faces up stage.)* Is it there now?

GUDGEON. To the best of my belief, sir. I can easily ascertain.

INSPECTOR. *(moving to left of the sofa and taking the revolver from his pocket)* It wasn't – this gun?

GUDGEON. *(moving in to left of the* INSPECTOR *and looking at the revolver)* Oh no, sir. That's a thirty-eight Smith and Wesson – this was a small pistol – a Derringer.

INSPECTOR. You seem to know a good deal about firearms.

GUDGEON. I served in the nineteen-fourteen-eighteen war, sir.

INSPECTOR. *(turning and moving down right)* And you say you found this Derringer pistol – on the oak chest in the hall?

GUDGEON. Yes, sir.

*(*LADY ANGKATELL *enters up centre from left. The* INSPECTOR *eases above the right end of the sofa.)*

LADY ANGKATELL. *(moving centre)* How nice to see you, Mr. Colquhoun. What is all this about a pistol and Gudgeon? I found that child Doris in floods of tears. The girl was quite right to say what she saw if she thought she saw it. I find right and wrong bewildering myself – easy when wrong is pleasant and right is unpleasant – but confusing the other way about, if you know what I mean. And what have you been telling them about this pistol, Gudgeon?

GUDGEON. *(respectfully but emphatically)* I found the pistol in the hall, m'lady. I have no idea who put it there. I picked it up and put it back in its proper place. That is what I have told the Inspector and he quite understands.

LADY ANGKATELL. *(gently shaking her head at* **GUDGEON***)* You shouldn't have done that, Gudgeon. I'll talk to the Inspector myself.

GUDGEON. But…

LADY ANGKATELL. I appreciate your motives, Gudgeon. I know you always try to save us trouble and annoyance. *(firmly)* That will do now.

(**GUDGEON** *hesitates, throws a quick glance at* **SIR HENRY**, *then bows and exits left.* **SIR HENRY** *looks very grave.)*

(**LADY ANGKATELL** *crosses to the sofa, sits and smiles disarmingly at the* **INSPECTOR**.*)*

LADY ANGKATELL. That was really very charming of Gudgeon. Quite feudal, if you know what I mean. Yes, feudal is the right word.

INSPECTOR. Am I to understand, Lady Angkatell, that you yourself have some further knowledge about the matter?

LADY ANGKATELL. Of course. Gudgeon didn't find the gun in the hall at all. He found it when he took the eggs out.

INSPECTOR. The eggs?

LADY ANGKATELL. Yes, out of the basket. *(She seems to think all is now explained.)*

SIR HENRY. You must tell us a little more, my dear. Inspector Colquhoun and I are still at sea.

LADY ANGKATELL. Oh! The gun, you see, was *in* the basket—

(SIR HENRY rises.)

– *under* the eggs.

INSPECTOR. What basket? And what eggs, Lady Angkatell?

LADY ANGKATELL. The basket I took down to the farm. The gun was in it and I put the eggs in on top of the gun and forgot about it. When we found poor John Cristow shot in here, it was such a shock that I let go the basket and Gudgeon caught it just in time – because of the eggs.

(SIR HENRY moves slowly to the fireplace.)

Later I asked him about writing the date on the eggs – so that one shouldn't eat the fresh ones before the old ones – and he said all that had already been attended to – and I remember now he was rather emphatic about it. He found the gun, you see, and put it back in Henry's study. Very nice and loyal of him – but also very foolish, because, of course, Inspector, the truth is what you want to hear, isn't it?

INSPECTOR. *(crossing above the sofa to centre; grimly)* The truth is what I mean to get.

LADY ANGKATELL. *Of course.* It's all so sad, all this hounding people.

(The INSPECTOR moves to left of the sofa.)

I don't suppose whoever it was that shot John Cristow really *meant* to shoot him.

(The INSPECTOR and the SERGEANT look at each other.)

LADY ANGKATELL. *(cont.)* – not seriously I mean. If it was Gerda, I'm quite sure she didn't. In fact, I'm rather surprised she didn't miss – it's the sort of thing one would expect of her.

(The INSPECTOR *crosses above the sofa to right.)*

If she did shoot him, she's probably dreadfully sorry about it now. It's bad enough for children having their father murdered, without having their mother hanged for it. *(accusingly)* I sometimes wonder if you policemen *think* of these things.

INSPECTOR. *(crossing below the sofa to left of it; taken aback)* We are not contemplating making an arrest just at present, Lady Angkatell.

LADY ANGKATELL. *(with a dazzling smile)* Well, that's sensible. But I have always felt that you are a very sensible man, Mr. Colquhoun.

INSPECTOR. Er – thank you, Lady Angkatell. *(He breaks up centre and turns.)* Now I want to get this clear. *(He moves down left centre.)* You had been shooting with this revolver?

LADY ANGKATELL. Pistol.

INSPECTOR. Ah yes, so Gudgeon said. You had been shooting with it at the targets?

LADY ANGKATELL. Oh, no, no. I took it out of Henry's study before I went to the farm.

INSPECTOR. *(looking at* SIR HENRY *and then at the armchair left centre)* May I?

*(*SIR HENRY *nods.)*

(He sits.) Why, Lady Angkatell?

LADY ANGKATELL. *(with unexpected triumph)* I knew you'd ask me that. And of course there must be some answer. *(She looks at* SIR HENRY.) Mustn't there, Henry?

SIR HENRY. I should certainly have thought so, my dear.

LADY ANGKATELL. Yes, obviously I must have had *some* idea in my head when I took that little Derringer and put it in my *egg* basket. *(She looks hopefully at* SIR HENRY.) I wonder what it could have been?

SIR HENRY. My wife is extremely absent-minded, Inspector.

INSPECTOR. So it seems.

LADY ANGKATELL. Why should I have taken that pistol?

INSPECTOR. *(rising and breaking up centre)* I haven't the faintest idea, Lady Angkatell.

LADY ANGKATELL. *(rising)* I came in *here* – this being your study, Henry – with the window there and the fireplace here. I had been talking to Simmonds about pillow cases – let's hang on to pillow cases – and I distinctly remember crossing – *(She moves to the writing table.)* over to the fireplace – and thinking we must get a new poker – the curate, not the rector – *(She looks at the* **INSPECTOR***.)* you're probably too young to know what that means.

(The **INSPECTOR** *and the* **SERGEANT** *look at each other.)*

And I remember opening the drawer and taking out the Derringer – it was a nice handy little gun – I've always liked it – and dropping it in the *egg* basket. And then I... No, there were so many things in my head – *(She eases to the sofa and sits.)* what with bindweed in the border – and hoping Mrs. Medway would make a really rich chocolate mousse.

SERGEANT. *(unable to contain himself)* A chocolate mousse?

LADY ANGKATELL. Yes, chocolate, eggs and cream. John Cristow loved a really rich sweet.

INSPECTOR. *(moving to left of the sofa)* Did you load the pistol?

LADY ANGKATELL. *(thoughtfully)* Ah, did I? Really, it's too ridiculous that I can't remember. But I should think I must have, don't you, Inspector?

INSPECTOR. I think I'll have a few more words with Gudgeon.

(He turns and crosses to the door left) When you remember a little more, perhaps you'll let me know, Lady Angkatell?

(The SERGEANT crosses to the door left.)

LADY ANGKATELL. Of course. Things come back to one quite suddenly sometimes, don't they?

INSPECTOR. Yes.

(He exits left. The SERGEANT follows him off. The clock strikes eleven.)

SIR HENRY. *(crossing to left of the sofa)* Why did you take the pistol, Lucy?

LADY ANGKATELL. I'm really not quite sure, Henry – I suppose I had some vague idea about an accident.

SIR HENRY. Accident?

LADY ANGKATELL. Yes, all those roots of tree sticking up – so easy to trip over one. I've always thought that an accident would be the simplest way to do a thing of that kind. One would be dreadfully sorry, of course, and blame oneself…

(Her voice trails off.)

SIR HENRY. Who was to have had the accident?

LADY ANGKATELL. John Cristow, of course.

SIR HENRY. *(sitting left of her on the sofa)* Good God, Lucy!

*(**LADY ANGKATELL**'s manner suddenly changes. All the vagueness goes and she is almost fanatical.)*

LADY ANGKATELL. Oh, Henry, I've been so dreadfully worried. About Ainswick.

SIR HENRY. I see. So it was Ainswick. You've always cared too much about Ainswick, Lucy.

LADY ANGKATELL. You and Edward are the last of the Angkatells. Unless Edward marries, the whole thing will die out – and he's so obstinate – that long head of his, just like my father. I felt that if only John were out of the way, Henrietta would marry Edward – she's really quite fond of him – and when a person's dead, you do forget. So, it all came to that – get rid of John Cristow.

SIR HENRY. *(aghast)* Lucy! It was you…

LADY ANGKATELL. *(her elusive self again)* Darling, darling, you don't imagine for a moment that *I* shot John? *(She laughs, rises, crosses to the fireplace and picks up the box of chocolates from the mantelpiece.)* I did have that silly idea about an accident. But then I remembered that he was our guest. *(She eases centre.)* One doesn't ask someone to be a guest and then get behind a bush and have a pop at them. *(She moves above the sofa and leans over the back of it.)* So you mustn't worry, Henry, any more.

SIR HENRY. *(hoarsely)* I always worry about you, Lucy.

LADY ANGKATELL. *(taking a chocolate from the box)* There's no need to, dear. *(She holds up the chocolate.)* Look what's coming. Open.

> *(**SIR HENRY** opens his mouth.)*

> *(She pops the chocolate into **SIR HENRY**'s mouth.)* There! John has been got rid of without our having to do anything about it. It reminds me of that man in Bombay who was so rude to me at a dinner party. *(She crosses to the window right)* Do you remember? Three days later he was run over by a tram.

> *(She exits right. The telephone rings. **SIR HENRY** rises, moves to the telephone and lifts the receiver.)*

OPERATOR. Your Regent call, sir.

SIR HENRY. *(into the telephone)* Hullo – yes – Regent call?

> *(**MIDGE** enters left.)*

MIDGE. For me?

SIR HENRY. Yes.

> *(**MIDGE** crosses to the telephone and takes the receiver from **SIR HENRY**, who exits right)*

MIDGE. *(into the telephone)* Hullo. Is that Madame?

VOICE. No, it's Vera.

MIDGE. Can I speak to Madame herself?

VOICE. Hold on, will you.

(There is a short pause, then another **VOICE** *is heard through the telephone.)*

VOICE. 'Allo. This is Madame Henri speaking.

MIDGE. It's Miss Harvey.

VOICE. Why are you not 'ere? You are coming back this afternoon, yes?

MIDGE. No, no, I'm afraid I can't come back this afternoon.

*(***EDWARD*** enters up centre from left and moves to left centre)*

VOICE. Oh, always these excuses.

MIDGE. No, no, it's not an excuse.

*(***EDWARD*** asks by a gesture whether she minds him staying.)*

(She puts her hand over the mouthpiece. To **EDWARD.***)* No – no, don't go. It's only my shop.

VOICE. What is it then?

MIDGE. *(into the telephone)* There's been an accident.

*(***EDWARD*** picks up a magazine from the coffee table, then sits on the sofa at the left end of it.)*

VOICE. An accident? Don't tell me these lies. Don't make these excuses.

MIDGE. No, I'm not telling you lies or making excuses. I can't come back today. I'm not allowed to leave. It's the police.

VOICE. The police?

MIDGE. Yes, the police.

VOICE. What 'ave you done?

MIDGE. It's not my fault. One can't help these things.

VOICE. Where are you?

MIDGE. I'm at Dowfield.

VOICE. Where there is a murder?

MIDGE. Yes, you read about it in the paper?

VOICE. Of course. This is most inconvenient. What do you think my customers will say when they know you are mixed up in a murder?

MIDGE. It's hardly my fault.

VOICE. It's all most upsetting.

MIDGE. Murder is.

VOICE. It's very exciting for you. Very nice for you to be in the limelight.

MIDGE. I think you are being rather unjust.

VOICE. If you do not return today, you will not 'ave any job. There are plenty of girls who would be 'appy to 'ave it.

MIDGE. Please don't say such things. I'm very sorry.

VOICE. You will return tomorrow or don't dare to show your face again.

(**MIDGE** *replaces the receiver. She is near to tears.*)

EDWARD. Who was that?

MIDGE. My employer.

EDWARD. You should have told her to go to hell.

MIDGE. And get myself fired?

EDWARD. I can't bear to hear you so – subservient.

MIDGE. You don't understand what you're talking about. *(She moves above the sofa.)* To show an independent spirit one needs an independent income.

EDWARD. My God, Midge, there are other jobs – interesting jobs.

MIDGE. Yes – you read advertisements asking for them every day in *The Times*.

EDWARD. Yes.

MIDGE. *(moving up centre)* Sometimes, Edward, you make me lose my temper. What do you know about jobs? Getting them and keeping them? This job, as it happens, is fairly well paid, with reasonable hours.

EDWARD. Oh, money!

MIDGE. *(moving to left of the sofa)* Yes, money. That's what I use to live on. I've got to have a job that *keeps* me, do you understand.

EDWARD. Henry and Lucy would...

MIDGE. We've been into that before. Of course they would. *(She crosses to the fireplace.)* It's no good, Edward. You're an Angkatell and Henry and Lucy are Angkatells, but I'm only half an Angkatell. My father was a plain little business man – honest and hardworking and probably not very clever. It's from him I get the feeling I don't like to accept favours. When his business failed, his creditors got paid twenty shillings in the pound. I'm like him. I mind about money and about debts. Don't you see, Edward, it's all right for you and Lucy. Lucy would have any of her friends to stay indefinitely and never think about it twice – and she could go and live on her friends if necessary. There would be no feeling of obligation. But I'm different.

EDWARD. *(rising)* You dear ridiculous child. *(He puts the magazine in the coffee table.)*

MIDGE. I may be ridiculous but *I am not a child.*

EDWARD. *(crossing to the fireplace and standing above* **MIDGE***)* But it's all wrong that you should have to put up with rudeness and insolence. My God, Midge, I'd like to take you out of it all – carry you off to Ainswick.

MIDGE. *(furiously and half crying)* Why do you say these stupid things? You don't mean them. *(She sits on the pouffe.)* Do you think it makes life any easier when I'm being bullied and shouted at to remember that there are places like Ainswick in the world? Do you think I'm grateful to you for standing there and babbling about how much you'd like to take me out of it all? It sounds so charming and means absolutely nothing.

EDWARD. Midge!

MIDGE. Don't you know I'd sell my soul to be at Ainswick now, this minute? I love Ainswick so much I can hardly bear to think of it. You're cruel, Edward, saying nice things you don't mean.

EDWARD. But I do mean them. *(He eases centre, turns and faces* **MIDGE**.*)* Come on, Midge. We'll drive to Ainswick now in my car.

MIDGE. Edward!

EDWARD. *(drawing* **MIDGE** *to her feet)* Come on, Midge. We're going to Ainswick. Shall we? What about it, eh?

MIDGE. *(laughing a little hysterically)* I've called your bluff, haven't I?

EDWARD. It isn't bluff.

MIDGE. *(patting* **EDWARD**'s *arm then crossing to left of the sofa)* Calm down, Edward. In any case, the police would stop us.

EDWARD. Yes, I suppose they would.

MIDGE. *(sitting on the sofa at the left end of it; gently)* All right, Edward, I'm sorry I shouted at you.

EDWARD. *(quietly)* You really love Ainswick, don't you?

MIDGE. I'm resigned to not going there, but don't rub it in.

EDWARD. I can see it wouldn't do to rush off there this moment – *(he moves to left of the sofa)* but I'm suggesting that you come to Ainswick for good.

MIDGE. For good?

EDWARD. I'm suggesting that you marry me, Midge.

MIDGE. Marry...?

EDWARD. I'm not a very romantic proposition. I'm a dull dog. I read what I expect you would think are dull books, and I write a few dull articles and potter about the estate. But we've known each other a long time – and perhaps Ainswick would make up for me. Will you come, Midge?

MIDGE. *Marry* you? *(She rises.)*

EDWARD. Can you bear the idea?

MIDGE. *(kneeling at the left end of the sofa and leaning over the end of it towards* **EDWARD**; *incoherently)* Edward, oh,

Edward – you offer me heaven like – like something on a plate.

(**EDWARD** *takes her hands and kisses them.* **LADY ANGKATELL** *enters right*)

LADY ANGKATELL. *(as she enters)* What I feel about rhododendrons is that unless you mass them in big clumps you don't get…

MIDGE. *(rising and turning to* **LADY ANGKATELL***)* Edward and I are going to be married.

LADY ANGKATELL. *(dumbfounded)* Married? You and Edward? But, Midge, I never dre— *(She recovers herself, moves to* **MIDGE***, kisses her, then holds out her hand to* **EDWARD***.)* Oh, darling, I'm so happy. *(She shakes* **EDWARD***'s hand and her face lights up.)* I am so delighted. You'll stay on here and give up that horrid shop. You can be married from here – Henry can give you away.

MIDGE. Darling Lucy, I'd love to be married from here.

LADY ANGKATELL. *(sitting on the sofa at the right end of it)* Off-white satin, and an ivory prayer book – no bouquet. Bridesmaids?

MIDGE. Oh no, I don't want any fuss.

EDWARD. Just a very quiet wedding, Lucy.

LADY ANGKATELL. Yes, I know exactly what you mean, darling. Unless one carefully chooses them, bridesmaids never match properly – there's nearly always one plain one who ruins the whole effect – usually the bridegroom's sister. And children – children are the worst of all. They step on the train, they howl for Nannie. I never feel a bride can go up the aisle in a proper frame of mind while she's so uncertain what's happening behind her.

MIDGE. I don't need to have anything behind me, not even a train. I can be married in a coat and skirt.

LADY ANGKATELL. *(rising and crossing left centre)* Oh no, Midge – that's too much like a widow. Off-white satin and I shall take you to Mireille.

MIDGE. I can't possibly afford Mireille.

LADY ANGKATELL. Darling, Henry and I will give you your trousseau.

MIDGE. *(crossing to* **LADY ANGKATELL** *and kissing her)* Darling. *(She turns, crosses to* **EDWARD** *and holds his hands.)*

LADY ANGKATELL. Dear Midge, dear Edward! I do hope that band on Henry's trousers won't be too tight. I'd like him to enjoy himself. As for me, I shall wear… *(She closes her eyes.)*

MIDGE. Yes, Lucy?

LADY ANGKATELL. Hydrangea blue – and silver fox. That's settled. What a pity John Cristow's dead. Really quite unnecessary after all. But what an exciting weekend. *(She moves to left of* **MIDGE** *and* **EDWARD.**) First a murder, then a marriage, then this, then that.

(The **INSPECTOR** *and the* **SERGEANT** *enter left.)*

(She turns.) Come in – come in. These young people have just got engaged to be married.

INSPECTOR. *(easing left centre)* Indeed. My congratulations.

EDWARD. Thank you very much.

LADY ANGKATELL. *(crossing to the door left)* I suppose I ought to get ready for the inquest. I am *so* looking forward to it. I've never been to an inquest before.

(She exits left. The **SERGEANT** *closes the door.* **EDWARD** *and* **MIDGE** *cross and exit right.)*

SERGEANT. *(crossing to right)* You may say what you like, she's a queer one. *(He nods towards the window right.)* And what about those two? So it was *her* he was keen on, and not the other one.

INSPECTOR. So it seems now.

SERGEANT. Well, that about washes him out. Who have we got left?

INSPECTOR. We've only got Gudgeon's word for it that the gun in Lady Angkatell's basket is what he says it was.

It's still wide open. You know, we've forgotten one thing, Penny – the holster.

SERGEANT. Holster?

INSPECTOR. Sir Henry told us that the gun was originally in a brown leather holster. Where's the holster?

(**SIR HENRY** *enters left.*)

SIR HENRY. I suppose we ought to be starting – (*He crosses to the windows right.*) but everyone seems to have disappeared for some extraordinary reason. (*He looks out of the window and calls.*) Edward. Midge.

(**LADY ANGKATELL** *enters left. She wears her hat and coat. She carries a prayer book and one white glove and one grey glove.*)

LADY ANGKATELL. (*moving left centre*) How do I look? Is this the sort of thing one wears?

SIR HENRY. (*turning and moving to right of the sofa*) You don't need a prayer book, my dear.

LADY ANGKATELL. But I thought one swore things.

INSPECTOR. Evidence isn't usually taken on oath in a coroner's court, Lady Angkatell. In any case, the proceedings will be purely formal today. (*He crosses to the door left.*)

(*The* **SERGEANT** *crosses to the door left.*)

Well, if you'll excuse me, we'll both be getting on our way.

(*He exits left. The* **SERGEANT** *follows him off.*)

LADY ANGKATELL. (*easing to the fireplace*) You and I and Gerda can go in the Daimler, and Edward can take Midge and Henrietta.

SIR HENRY. (*moving centre*) Where's Gerda?

LADY ANGKATELL. Henrietta is with her.

(**EDWARD** *and* **MIDGE** *enter right.* **MIDGE** *picks up her bag and gloves from the writing table, and moves below* *the sofa.* EDWARD *crosses above the sofa to right of* SIR HENRY.)

SIR HENRY. Well, what's this I hear about you two? *(He shakes hands with* EDWARD.*)* Isn't this wonderful news? *(He crosses to left of* MIDGE *and kisses her.)*

EDWARD. Thank you, Henry.

MIDGE. Thank you, Cousin Henry.

LADY ANGKATELL. *(looking at her gloves)* Now what made me take one white glove and one grey glove? How very odd.

(She exits left.)

EDWARD. *(moving up centre)* I'll get my car round.

(He exits up centre to left.)

MIDGE. *(sitting on the sofa)* Are you really pleased?

SIR HENRY. It's the best news I've heard for a long time. You don't know what it'll mean to Lucy. She's got Ainswick on the brain, as you know.

MIDGE. She wanted Edward to marry Henrietta. *(troubled)* Will she mind that it's me?

SIR HENRY. Of course not. She only wanted Edward to marry. If you want my opinion, you'll make him a far better wife than Henrietta.

MIDGE. It's always been Henrietta with Edward.

SIR HENRY. *(crossing to the fireplace)* Well, don't you let those police fellows hear you say so. *(He fills his cigarette case from the box on the mantelpiece.)* Best thing in the world from that point of view that he's got engaged to you. Takes suspicion right off him.

MIDGE. *(rising)* Suspicion? Off Edward?

SIR HENRY. *(turning)* Counting Gerda out of it, I should say he was suspect number one. To put it bluntly, he loathed John Cristow's guts.

MIDGE. *(crossing to centre then moving up left)* I remember – the evening after the murder – so that's why... *(Her face grows desperately unhappy.)*

(**HENRIETTA** *enters left.*)

HENRIETTA. Oh, Henry, I'm taking Gerda with me. *(She crosses to the drinks table and picks up her gloves and bag.)* She is in rather a nervous state – and I think that one of Lucy's conversations would just about finish her. We're starting now.

SIR HENRY. *(moving to the door left)* Yes, we ought to be starting too.

(He exits left, leaving the door open.)

(Off; calling.) Are you ready, Lucy?

HENRIETTA. *(putting on her gloves)* Congratulations, Midge. Did you stand on a table and shout at him?

MIDGE. *(solemnly)* I rather think I did.

HENRIETTA. I told you that was what Edward needed.

MIDGE. *(moving to the radio)* I don't think Edward will ever *really* love anyone but you.

HENRIETTA. Oh, don't be absurd, Midge.

MIDGE. I'm not absurd. It's the sort of thing one – knows.

HENRIETTA. Edward wouldn't ask you to marry him unless he wanted to.

MIDGE. *(switching on the radio)* He may have thought it – wise.

HENRIETTA. What do you mean?

GERDA. *(off left; calling)* Henrietta.

HENRIETTA. *(crossing to the door left)* I'm coming, Gerda.

*(She exits left. The radio warms up and music is heard. The tune is "La Fille aux Cheveux de Lin." **MIDGE** moves to the fireplace, puts her gloves on the mantelpiece and looks in the mirror. **EDWARD** enters up centre from left.)*

EDWARD. *(moving left centre)* The car's outside.

MIDGE. *(turning)* If you don't mind, I'll go with Lucy.

EDWARD. But why…?

MIDGE. She loses things – and flutters – I'll be useful. *(She moves down left.)*

EDWARD. *(hurt)* Midge, is anything the matter? What is it?

MIDGE. *(crossing to right)* Never mind now. We must get to the inquest.

EDWARD. Something *is* the matter.

MIDGE. Don't – don't bother me.

EDWARD. Midge, have you changed your mind? Did I – rush you into things just now? *(He moves below the sofa.)* You don't want to marry me after all?

MIDGE. No, no – we must keep on with it now. Until all this is over.

EDWARD. What do you mean?

MIDGE. As things are – it's better you should be engaged to me. Later, we can break it off. *(She turns her back to him.)*

(EDWARD looks stunned for a moment, then controls himself and speaks in a monotone.)

EDWARD. I see – even for Ainswick – you can't go through with it.

MIDGE. *(turning)* It wouldn't work, Edward.

EDWARD. No, I suppose you are right. *(He turns and faces up left.)* You'd better go. The others will be waiting.

MIDGE. Aren't you...?

EDWARD. I'll be along. I'm used to driving alone.

(MIDGE exits up centre to left. EDWARD crosses and exits left. After a few moments, he re-enters. He carries a revolver. He closes the door, crosses to the radio and switches it off, moves to the fireplace, picks up MIDGE's gloves from the mantelpiece and puts them in his pocket. He then moves left centre and opens the revolver to see if it is loaded. As he snaps the revolver shut, MIDGE enters up centre from left.)

MIDGE. Edward – are you still here?

EDWARD. *(striving to appear natural)* Why, Midge, you startled me.

MIDGE. *(moving above the sofa)* I came back for my gloves.

(She leans over the back of the sofa and looks under the cushions.)

I left them somewhere. *(She looks towards the mantelpiece and sees the revolver in* **EDWARD**'s *hand.)* Edward, what are you doing with that revolver?

EDWARD. I thought I might have a shot or two down at the targets.

MIDGE. At the targets? But there's the inquest.

EDWARD. The inquest, yes, of course. I forgot.

MIDGE. *(with a step towards him)* Edward – what is it? *(She moves in to right of him.)* My God! *(She snatches the gun from him, crosses to the mantelpiece.)* Give me that revolver – you must be mad. *(She puts the revolver on the up stage end of the mantelpiece.)*

*(***EDWARD** *sits in the armchair left centre.)*

(She turns.) How could you? *(She kneels down left of* **EDWARD**.*)* But why, Edward, but why? Because of Henrietta?

EDWARD. *(surprised),* Henrietta? No. That's all over now.

MIDGE. Why – tell me why?

EDWARD. It's all so hopeless.

MIDGE. Tell me, darling. Make me understand.

EDWARD. I'm no good, Midge. Never any good. It's men like Cristow – they're successful – women admire them. But I… Even for Ainswick you couldn't bring yourself to marry me.

MIDGE. You thought I was marrying you for Ainswick?

EDWARD. Heaven on a plate – but you couldn't face the prospect of having me thrown in.

MIDGE. That's not true, that's not true. Oh, you fool! Don't you understand? It was you I wanted, not Ainswick. I adore you – I've always adored you. I've loved you ever since I can remember. I've been sick with love for you sometimes.

EDWARD. You love *me?*

MIDGE. Of course I love you, you darling idiot. When you asked me to marry you I was in heaven.

EDWARD. But then why…?

MIDGE. I was a fool. I got it into my head you were doing it because of the police.

EDWARD. The police?

MIDGE. I thought – perhaps – you'd killed John Cristow.

EDWARD. I…?

MIDGE. For Henrietta – and I thought you'd got engaged to me to throw them off the scent. Oh, I must have been crazy. *(She rises.)*

EDWARD. *(rising)* I can't say I'm sorry that Cristow is dead – *(He crosses to the fireplace.)* but I should never have dreamed of killing him.

MIDGE. *(moving in to right of him)* I know. I'm a fool. *(She lays her head on his chest.)* But I was so jealous of Henrietta.

EDWARD. *(putting his arms around her)* You needn't be, Midge. It was Henrietta, the girl, I loved. But that day you lit the fire for me, I realized Henrietta the woman was a stranger I didn't know. When you asked me to look at you, I saw you for the first time, not Midge the little girl, but Midge the woman – warm and alive.

MIDGE. Oh, Edward.

EDWARD. Midge, don't ever leave me again.

MIDGE. Never. I promise you never.

(The sound of a motor horn is heard up centre.)

Heavens, Edward, we must go. They're waiting. What did I come back for? Gloves!

(EDWARD takes MIDGE's gloves from his pocket and holds them out to her.)

Oh, darling!

*(She lakes the gloves from him, turns and exit's up
centre to left.* **EDWARD** *follows her off. The lights fade
to a blackout, during which the alcove curtain is closed.
There is a pause of six seconds then the lights come up.
One hour is presumed to have elapsed, during which
the weather has turned stormy and the sky is overcast.*
GERDA *and* **HENRIETTA** *enter up centre from left.*
HENRIETTA *is supporting* **GERDA***. They both carry
handbags.)*

HENRIETTA. *(as she enters)* We've beaten the storm. Good
heavens, it's as dark as night in here. *(As she passes the
drinks table she switches on the lamp.)* Are you all right?
Sure? *(She leads* **GERDA** *to the sofa.)* Come over here and
put your feet up. *(She puts her handbag on the writing
table.)*

*(***GERDA** *sits on the sofa at the left end of it.* **HENRIETTA**
moves to the drinks table.)

GERDA. I'm so sorry to give so much trouble. I can't think
why I felt faint.

HENRIETTA. *(pouring out a brandy and water)* Anyone might,
it was very stuffy in that place.

GERDA. I hope I gave my evidence all right. I get so
confused.

HENRIETTA. You did very well indeed.

GERDA. The coroner was so very kind. Oh dear, I'm so glad
it's all over. If only my head didn't ache so.

HENRIETTA. *(picking up the drink and moving below the sofa)*
You need a drink. *(She holds out the glass to* **GERDA***.)*

GERDA. Oh no, thank you, not for me.

HENRIETTA. Well, *I* need one. You'd much better have one
too.

GERDA. No – really.

*(***HENRIETTA** *moves to the drinks table, takes a sip from
the glass, then stands it on the table.)*

What I would love— but perhaps it would be giving a
lot of trouble…

HENRIETTA. *(moving to right of the sofa)* Get the idea of giving trouble out of your head, Gerda. What would you like so much?

GERDA. I'd love some tea – a nice cup of hot tea.

HENRIETTA. *(crossing to left centre)* Of course.

GERDA. But it is a trouble. The servants...

HENRIETTA. *(crossing to the fireplace)* That's all right. *(She stretches out a hand towards the bell-push, then stops.)* Oh, I forgot, Gudgeon's at the inquest.

GERDA. It doesn't matter.

HENRIETTA. I'll go down to the kitchen and ask Mrs. Medway.

GERDA. She might not like being asked.

HENRIETTA. She won't mind. She mightn't have liked answering a bell.

GERDA. You're very good to me.

(HENRIETTA exits left There is a flash of lightning followed by a peal of thunder. GERDA rises, startled, crosses to the windows right, glances out, moves up centre, then turns, moves left centre and looks horror-struck at the spot where JOHN died. She catches her breath, crosses to the sofa, sits and starts to cry quietly.)

Oh, John – John – I can't bear it.

(HENRIETTA enters left.)

HENRIETTA. The kettle's on – only be a moment. *(She crosses to left of the sofa. Gently)* Oh – Gerda, don't cry. It's all over now.

GERDA. But what shall I do? What can I do without John?

HENRIETTA. There are the children.

GERDA. I know, I know. But John always decided everything.

HENRIETTA. I know. *(She hesitates a moment, then moves above the sofa, puts her hands on GERDA's shoulders, and draws her back on the sofa.)* There's just one thing, Gerda. *(She pauses.)* What did you do with the holster?

GERDA. *(staring front)* Holster?

HENRIETTA. The second revolver, the one you took from Henry's study, was in a holster. What have you done with the holster?

GERDA. *(repeating the word with an appearance of stupidity)* Holster?

HENRIETTA. *(urgently)* You must tell me. Apart from that everything's all right. There's nothing else that can possibly give you away. They may suspect – but they can't prove anything. But that holster's dangerous. Have you still got it?

(GERDA slowly nods her head.)

Where is it?

GERDA. I cut it up in pieces and put it in my leathercraft bag.

HENRIETTA. *(moving to the drinks table and picking up the leathercraft bag)* In this?

(GERDA turns and nods.)

(She moves to the writing table, switches on the table-lamp, then takes some pieces of brown leather out of the leathercraft bag.) I'll take and get rid of them. *(She puts them in her own handbag.)* Quite a clever idea of yours.

(GERDA, for the first time, speaks in a high, excited voice and shows that she is not quite sane.)

GERDA. I'm not so stupid as people think. When did you know that I shot John?

HENRIETTA. *(putting the bags on the writing table)* I've always known. *(She moves to right of the sofa.)* When John said "Henrietta" to me just before he died, I knew what he meant. I always knew what John wanted. He wanted me to protect you – to keep you out of it somehow. He loved you very much. He loved you better than he knew.

GERDA. *(weeping)* Oh, John – John.

HENRIETTA. *(sitting right of* GERDA *on the sofa)* I know, my dear. I know. *(She puts her arm around* GERDA.*)*

GERDA. But you can't know. It was all a lie – everything. I *had* to kill him. I'd adored him so. I worshipped him. I thought he was everything that was noble and fine. He wasn't any of those things.

HENRIETTA. He was a man – not a god.

GERDA. *(fiercely)* It was all a lie. The night when that woman came here – that film woman. I saw his face as he looked at her. And after dinner he went over to see her. He didn't come back. I went up to bed, but I couldn't sleep. Hour after hour – he didn't come. At last I got up and put on a coat and my shoes and I crept downstairs and through the side door. I went along the lane to her cottage. The curtains were drawn at the front but I went round to the back. They weren't drawn there because I crept up to the window and looked in. *(Her voice rises hysterically.)* I looked in.

(There is a flash of lightning and a distant peal of thunder.)

HENRIETTA. *(rising)* Gerda!

GERDA. I saw them – that woman and John. *(She pauses.)* I saw them. *(She pauses.)* I'd believed in John – completely – utterly – and it was all a lie. I was left with nothing – nothing. *(She suddenly resumes a quiet conversational tone.)* You do see, don't you, Henrietta, that I had to kill him? *(She pauses.)* Is that tea coming? I do so want a cup of tea.

HENRIETTA. *(moving above the right end of the sofa)* In a moment. Go on telling me, Gerda.

GERDA. *(cunningly)* They always said I was stupid when I was a child – stupid and slow. They used to say, "Don't let Gerda do it, Gerda will take all day." And sometimes, "Gerda never seems to take in anything you say to her." Didn't they see, all of them, that that made me more stupid and slower still? And then you know – I found a way. I used to pretend to be stupider than

I was. I'd stare as though I didn't understand. But inside, sometimes, I laughed. Because often I knew more than they thought.

HENRIETTA. *(moving to left of the sofa)* I see – yes, I see.

GERDA. John didn't mind my being stupid – not at first. He used to tell me not to worry – to leave everything to him. Only when he was very busy he got impatient. And sometimes I used to think I couldn't do anything right. Then I'd remember how clever he was – and how good. Only – after all, he wasn't – so I had to kill him.

HENRIETTA. Go on.

GERDA. I knew I must be careful because the police are very clever. I read in a detective story that they could tell which revolver a bullet had been fired from. So I took a second revolver from Henry's study and I shot John with that, and dropped the other by him. Then I ran round the house, in at the front door and through that door and over to John and picked the revolver up. I thought, you see, that first they'd think I had done it, and then they'd find that it wasn't the right revolver and so I'd be cleared. And then I meant to put the revolver that had shot him into that film woman's house and they'd think that *she'd* done it. Only she left her bag – so it was easier still. I slipped it into that later in the day. I can't think why they haven't arrested her. *(Her voice rises.)* They should have. *(hysterically)* It was because of her I had to kill John.

HENRIETTA. *(moving below the left end of the sofa)* You wiped your fingerprints off the second revolver you shot him with?

GERDA. Of course. I'm cleverer than people think. I got rid of the revolver. *(She frowns.)* But I did forget about the holster.

HENRIETTA. Don't worry about that. I've got it now. I think you're quite safe, Gerda. *(She sits left of **GERDA** on the* *sofa.)* You must go away and live in the country quietly somewhere – and forget.

GERDA. *(unhappily)* Yes, yes, I suppose I must. I don't know what to do. I don't really know where to go. I can't make up my mind – John always decided everything. My head aches.

HENRIETTA. *(rising)* I'll go and get the tea.

(She crosses and exits left. **GERDA** *looks cunningly towards the door left, rises, moves to the drinks table, takes a small poison bottle out of her handbag and stretches out her hand towards* **HENRIETTA** *'s glass. She pauses, takes a handkerchief from her handbag and lifts the glass with it.* **HENRIETTA** *re-enters quietly left She carries a tray of tea.* **GERDA,** *with her back to* **HENRIETTA,** *is unaware of the entry. As* **HENRIETTA** *watches,* **GERDA** *tips the contents of the poison bottle into* **HENRIETTA** *'s glass, then replaces the bottle and handkerchief in her handbag.* **HENRIETTA** *quietly exits.* **GERDA** *turns, moves below the sofa and sits.* **HENRIETTA** *re-enters, crosses to the coffee table and puts the tray on it.)*

Here's your tea, Gerda.

GERDA. Thank you so much, Henrietta.

HENRIETTA. *(moving to the drinks table)* Now, where's my drink? *(She picks up her glass.)*

GERDA. *(pouring milk into the cup)* This is just what I wanted. You are very good to me, Henrietta.

HENRIETTA. *(moving slowly down right)* Shall I have this? Or shall I have a cup of tea with you?

GERDA. *(pouring the tea; cunningly)* You don't really like tea, do you, Henrietta?

HENRIETTA. *(sharply)* I think, *today,* I prefer it. *(She puts her glass on the coffee table and crosses to the door left.)* I'll go and get another cup.

(She exits left. **GERDA** *frowns with annoyance, and rises. She looks around, sees the revolver on the mantelpiece, glances at the door left, then runs to the mantelpiece and*

picks up the revolver. She examines it, notes that it is loaded, nods with satisfaction and utters a little sob. The **INSPECTOR** *enters down right.)*

INSPECTOR. What are you doing with that gun, Mrs. Cristow?

GERDA. *(turning; startled)* Oh, Inspector, how you startled me. *(She puts her hand over her heart.)* My heart – my heart isn't strong, you know.

INSPECTOR. *(crossing to right of* **GERDA***)* What were you doing with that gun?

GERDA. I found it – here.

INSPECTOR. *(taking the revolver from* **GERDA***)* You know all about loading a gun, don't you? *(He unloads it, puts the cartridges in one pocket and the revolver in another.)*

GERDA. Sir Henry very kindly showed me. Is – is the inquest over?

INSPECTOR. Yes.

GERDA. And the verdict?

INSPECTOR. It was adjourned.

GERDA. That's not right. They should have said it was wilful murder and that she did it.

INSPECTOR. She?

GERDA. That actress. That Veronica Craye. If they adjourn things, she'll get away – she'll go back to America.

INSPECTOR. Veronica Craye didn't shoot your husband, Mrs. Cristow.

GERDA. She did. She did. Of course she did.

INSPECTOR. No. The gun wasn't in her bag when we first searched this room. It was put there afterwards. *(He pauses.)* We often know quite well who's guilty of crime, Mrs. Cristow – *(he looks meaningly at her)* but we can't always get sufficient evidence.

*(***GERDA***, terrified, steps back, stumbles and collapses on to the pouffe.)*

GERDA. *(wildly)* Oh, John – John – where are you? I want you, John.

INSPECTOR. Mrs. Cristow – Mrs. Cristow – don't – don't, please.

*(**GERDA** sobs hysterically. The **INSPECTOR** crosses to the coffee table, picks up **HENRIETTA**'s glass, sniffs it, takes it to **GERDA** and hands it to her. **GERDA**, not noticing what it is, drinks the contents of the glass. After a few moments, she rises, staggers and crosses below the sofa. As she starts to fall the **INSPECTOR** crosses to her and lowers her on to the sofa. **HENRIETTA** enters left. She carries a cup and saucer. She crosses hurriedly to left. of the sofa, kneeling and putting the cup and saucer on the coffee table, as the **INSPECTOR** takes the empty glass from **GERDA**.)*

HENRIETTA. Gerda, Gerda. *(She sees the glass. To the* **INSPECTOR**.*)* Did you – did you give her *that?*

INSPECTOR. Why, what was in it?

HENRIETTA. She put something in it – out of her bag.

(The **INSPECTOR** *picks up* **GERDA***'s handbag, opens it and takes out the poison bottle.)*

INSPECTOR. *(reading the label)* I wonder how she got hold of that? *(He feels* **GERDA***'s pulse then shakes his head.)* So – she's killed herself.

HENRIETTA. *(rising and crossing to right)* No, it was meant for me.

INSPECTOR. For *you,* why?

HENRIETTA. Because I – I knew – something. *(She crosses above the sofa to the back of the armchair centre.)*

INSPECTOR. You knew she'd killed her husband? Oh yes, *I* knew that too. We get to know people in our job. You're not the killer type. She was.

HENRIETTA. *(breaking to the fireplace)* She loved John Cristow – too much.

INSPECTOR. The worshipper – that was the name of the statue, wasn't it? What happens next for you?

HENRIETTA. John told me once that if he were dead, the first thing I'd do would be to model a figure of grief. It's odd, but that's exactly what I'm going to do.

(The INSPECTOR moves to the writing table. LADY ANGKATELL enters up centre from left. She looks radiant.)

LADY AKGKATELL. *(moving down centre)* It was a wonderful inquest.

(The INSPECTOR lifts the telephone receiver.)

Exactly as they describe it in books, and… *(She sees GERDA.)*
Has – has Gerda…?

(The INSPECTOR looks at her in silence. HENRIETTA puts her hands to her eyes to hide her tears.)

(She nods her head.) How very very fortunate…

INSPECTOR. *(into the telephone)* Get me the police station, will you?

(HENRIETTA *starts to sob as – the curtain falls)*

SET DESIGN

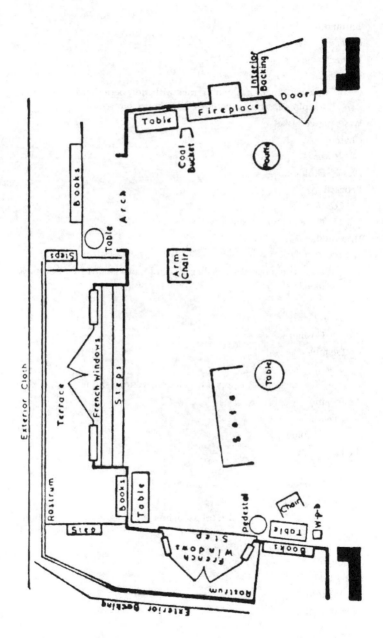

FURNITURE AND PROPERTY PLOT

Throughout the play:

Onstage:

Writing table.

> *On it:*
>
>> Inkstand, pen, notepaper rack with notepaper and envelopes, telephone, ashtray, matches, table-lamp, blotter.

Waste-paper basket.

Chair.

> *On it:*
>
>> Cushion.

Pedestal.

> *On it:*
>
>> Piece of abstract statuary.

Drinks table.

> *On it:*
>
>> Box with cigarettes, ashtray, book, table-lamp, 2 boxes of matches.

Sofa.

> *On it:*
>
>> Cushions.

Coffee table.

> *On it:*
>
>> Magazines, newspapers, box with cigarettes, ashtray.

Armchair.

> *On it:*
>
>> Cushion.

Table.

> *On it:*
>
>> Wireless receiver.

> *On mantelpiece:*
>
>> Clock, tobacco jar with tobacco, box with cigarettes, table lighter, 2 ashtrays, matches, small standing mirror, small statue, pair of electric candle-lamps.

Fender.

Fire-irons.

Coal-scuttle.

Hearth-rug.

Pouffe.

Over mantelpiece:

Picture of Ainswick House.

Carpet on floor.

Curtains at windows.

Miniatures on walls.

Light switch below fireplace.

Bell-push below fireplace.

Pitted bookshelves with books.

2 wall vases with flowers right and left of french windows up centre

In alcove:

Fitted bookshelves with books.

Table.

On it:

Silver bowl of roses.

On terrace up centre:

Hydrangea in pot.

Curtain in alcove arch.

Light switch right of alcove arch.

ACT ONE

Set.   *On terrace:*

Sculptor's stand.

On it:

Unfinished clay statue, piece of damp rag, piece of clay.

In ashtray on table down right:

Cigarette ends.

On sofa:

Copies of the *Daily Graphic* and *The Times*.

In ashtray on coffee table:

Cigarette ends.

On coffee table:

Small piece of clay.

In ashtrays on mantelpiece:

Cigarette ends.

On mantelpiece:

Mole-trap.

French windows open.

Alcove curtain closed.

Fire out.

Offstage:

> Suitcase (MIDGE)
>
> Empty flower-pot (LADY ANGKATELL)
>
> Lobster (LADY ANGKATELL)
>
> Salver (GUDGEON)
>
> Tray. *On it:* bottle of Martini, bottle of gin, decanter of sherry, cocktail mixing jug and spoon, 8 glasses, bowl of olives, tea-cloth (GUDGEON)
>
> Statuette (HENRIETTA)
>
> Packet of matches (GUDGEON)

Personal:

> SIR HENRY: pipe.
>
> MIDGE: gloves, handbag.
>
> EDWARD: case with cigarettes, lighter.
>
> VERONICA: "diamante" bag.
>
> GERDA: handbag, gloves.
>
> JOHN: case with cigarettes, lighter.
>
> HENRIETTA: handkerchief.

ACT TWO

Scene I

Strike:

> Glasses, tray of drinks, olives.
>
> Sculptor's stand.
>
> Flower-pot.
>
> Newspapers.

Set:

> *On coffee table:*
>
> > *Daily Mirror.*
> >
> > Blue vase.
>
> *On drinks table:*
>
> > White vase.
> >
> > Box with chocolates.
> >
> > Jug with water.

French windows open.

Alcove curtain closed.

Fire out.

Offstage:

> Salver.
>> *On it:* note (GUDGEON)
>
>> Dahlias and loose leaves (MIDGE)
>> Basket of eggs (LADY ANGKATBLL)
>> 2 revolvers (SIR HENRY)
>> Leathercraft bag (GERDA)

Personal:

> JOHN: wrist-watch, case with cigarettes, lighter.
> VERONICA: red suede handbag, *In it:* lighter.

Scene II

Strike:

> *Daily Mirror.*
> Empty vase.
> Book from sofa.

Set:

> *On drinks table:*
>> Tray. *On it:* decanter with brandy, jug of water, 4 glasses.
>
> *On writing table:*
>> MIDGE's handbag. *In it:* case with cigarettes.
>
> *On armchair left centre:*
>> Copy of *The Times,* pencil.
>
> *On sofa:*
>> Knitting.
>
> *Under cushion at left end of sofa:*
>> VERONICA's red handbag. *In it:* revolver.

Right window of french windows up centre open.

Left window of french windows up centre closed.

French windows right closed.

Alcove curtain closed.

Fire out.

Offstage:

> Tray. *On it:* pot with coffee, jug with milk, bowl with sugar, plate of sandwiches, 4 each cups, saucers and spoons (GUDGEON)
> Leathercraft bag (GERDA)
> Crumpled note (SERGEANT)

Personal:

SERGEANT: notebook and pencil.

EDWARD: handkerchief.

SIR HENRY: filled pipe, matches.

INSPECTOR: case with cigarettes, lighter, handkerchief.

ACT THREE

Strike:

Vase of dahlias.

MIDGE's handbag.

Set:

On mantelpiece:

Box with chocolates.

On coffee table:

Magazine.

On drinks table:

HENRIETTA's handbag and gloves.

GERDA's leathercraft bag. *In it:* Pieces of brown leather. Vase of flowers.

Down right:

Waste-paper basket.

French windows open.

Alcove curtains open.

Fire on.

Offstage:

Suitcase (MIDGE)

Prayer book, one white glove, one grey glove (LADY ANGKATELL)

Revolver (EDWARD)

Tray. *On it:* pot with tea, jug with milk, bowl with sugar, cup, saucer and spoon (HENRIETTA)

Cup and saucer (HENRIETTA)

Personal:

MIDGE: gloves, handbag.

INSPECTOR: revolver.

SIR HENRY: empty cigarette case.

HENRIETTA: handbag.

GERDA: handbag. *In it:* poison bottle, handkerchief.